She brushed th met his eyes.

Gunnar had to admit, whatever she'd gone through with that idiot ex of hers, she was a force of nature.

The press was still relentless in their pursuit of him. There was always a story about every woman he was seen with. Hopefully, the vultures wouldn't get to her, too. All the more reason to be very careful.

"How are you doing?" he asked her, over the whir of the helicopter blades.

"I'm good," she said.

He nodded. It was shameful how much he'd wanted to kiss her in the hot tub the other night. He'd almost made a move. Maybe he would've done, if she hadn't mentioned that she wanted a family. That had snapped him back to his senses. Not only was taking a colleague to his private retreat the kind of behavior to get everyone talking more nonsense about him, but he would never have children. She was too special a person to be fling material and too vulnerable to involve in all his family drama when she was trying to rebuild her own life.

He'd made the right decision backing off.

Dear Reader,

Welcome to one of my favorite stories yet! I always wanted to set a book in Iceland, one of my absolute favorite destinations ever. Years ago I was lucky enough to have an Icelandic boyfriend (briefly!) who took me there twice, once in summer and once in winter, and I got to see the real Iceland: the people, the culture, the love of music, the astonishing amount of homemade moonshine and the northern lights. All of it made it into this story, as experienced by our hero and heroine, although there's a little more action and drama to endure here, thanks to their troubled pasts and their search and rescue missions in the midst of all the blizzards. How will they even warm up enough to feel that first kiss?

Make yourself a hot drink and find out! Enjoy the journey…

Becky

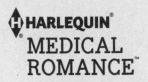

HARLEQUIN®
MEDICAL
ROMANCE™

Recycling programs
for this product may
not exist in your area.

ISBN-13: 978-1-335-59526-3

Melting the Surgeon's Heart

Harlequin Enterprises ULC
22 Adelaide St. West, 41st Floor
Toronto, Ontario M5H 4E3, Canada
www.Harlequin.com

Printed in U.S.A.

MELTING THE SURGEON'S HEART

BECKY WICKS

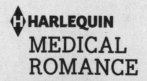
HARLEQUIN
MEDICAL
ROMANCE

Born in the UK, **Becky Wicks** has suffered interminable wanderlust from an early age. She's lived and worked all over the world, from London to Dubai, Sydney, Bali, NYC and Amsterdam. She's written for the likes of *GQ*, *Hello!*, *Fabulous* and *Time Out*, a host of YA romance, plus three travel memoirs—*Burqalicious*, *Balilicious* and *Latinalicious* (HarperCollins, Australia). Now she blends travel with romance for Harlequin and loves every minute! Tweet her @bex_wicks and subscribe at beckywicks.com.

Books by Becky Wicks

Harlequin Medical Romance

From Doctor to Daddy
Enticed by Her Island Billionaire
Falling Again for the Animal Whisperer
Fling with the Children's Heart Doctor
White Christmas with Her Millionaire Doc
A Princess in Naples
The Vet's Escape to Paradise
Highland Fling with Her Best Friend
South African Escape to Heal Her
Finding Forever with the Single Dad

Visit the Author Profile page
at Harlequin.com for more titles.

Dedicated to the Icelanders
who always made me feel at home.

Praise for
Becky Wicks

"A fast paced, beautifully set and heart warming medical romance set in the stunning Galapagos Islands. Interwoven with a conservation theme which is clearly a passion of the author."
—*Harlequin Junkie* on *The Vet's Escape to Paradise*

CHAPTER ONE

THE SNOWSTORM SEETHED with the ferocity of a wild beast as Mahlia strode with her face down, her hair whipping violently around her face. Flakes of snow the size of boulders flew past the rim of her hood like an unrelenting army under the sinister sky and she shivered, knowing her chapped lips were probably turning a deathly shade of blue. No sign of the northern lights tonight, she thought. If they were up there somewhere, they were hiding away in fear of this storm.

Even as an experienced search and rescue paramedic, it was hard for her not to fear the unknown out here in Iceland. She was fast becoming a snowman. A snow*woman*. One who could easily merge with a snowdrift and never be seen again.

Leaning into the wind, she trudged through the snow, wrapping her arms around herself, shivering. Just over a month in the country and already the New Zealand sun felt like a distant memory.

'Almost there,' her search team leader Erik called from ahead, where he was walking with Ásta, their search technician.

Mahlia's breath caught in her throat as a row of buildings suddenly emerged from the snowy mist. She quickened her pace, thoughts of hot chocolate and heat and light propelling her forward. The cold had long ago permeated through her thick coat and thermal trousers, and they'd only been following the compass from the road for fifteen minutes. The chopper would be with them as soon as it was safe to fly, and then they could recommence the search.

Inside the warm hut, she drew back her hood and shook out her mass of corkscrew curls. She caught a glimpse of her reflection in the window and frowned. Her lips were indeed an eerie shade of alien grey.

'Drink?' A small, hunched woman beckoned her forward to the worn wooden table and chairs.

'Yes, please…thank you,' she said gratefully through her chattering teeth, taking a seat by the fire.

The flames reached upwards like spindly hands from the hearth, their bright orange light spilling over the walls and across the wooden ceiling. It was snug in here, cosy, like a warm hug after all that walking. She grasped her mug, sipped her drink, and was vaguely aware of the murmurs of her crew and the kindly villagers who'd taken them into the community centre.

They all knew about the search. There were places like this set up for the volunteers all over the Thingvellir National Park now. But the raging snowstorm outside only served to heighten her discomfort and sense of dread. It was nearly two days since the Cessna plane carrying a male pilot in his mid-forties and two Swedish tourists in their thirties had gone missing. Over three hundred search and rescue volunteers had taken part in the search yesterday and over a hundred more had got on the case this morning. Everywhere they searched, all they seemed to find was silence.

Hopefully it didn't show on their faces, but everyone here shared the same unspoken worry—what if this mission ended in failure? With each hour that passed, the chances of finding the missing people alive were getting slimmer and slimmer. It was almost impossible to believe that anyone could survive in freezing conditions like these for so long. Iceland's weather was brutal, unpredictable, and in the middle of storms like this one it felt like the kind of savage cold she imagined her mother must have felt consumed by during the darkest patches of her depression.

Thank goodness she was better now, Mahlia thought; well enough to survive the thought of her only daughter being all the way out here.

Mahlia was still deep in thought when the sound of the helicopter's thrumming blades burst through every crack in the hut like a torrent of falling water. The storm had subsided, and Sven had finally been able to land. She ran to the door ahead of the others, flinging it open.

Sven, their pilot, whom she'd been working with for three weeks already, was stepping from the cockpit, the blades above him spinning their way to a standstill. He squeezed her shoulder on his way past, motioning that they both had to get inside. The kind old lady was already waiting with more hot drinks. But there was another pair of feet on the ground now—someone else who'd just jumped from the helicopter and slammed the door behind him. Mahlia stared at the new winchman and felt herself draw a long, deep breath from some place inside her she hadn't known was there.

Was this Gunnar? He'd come to join their crew after Elias, Ásta's husband, had fallen awkwardly and broken his left femur yesterday. The poor guy was still in hospital in Reykjavik. Ásta had stayed on the search, at his insistence.

Mahlia realised she'd been holding her breath almost too long. *What?* She kept her eyes on him, pulling her jacket more tightly around herself. The man was striding straight towards her now. He was tall and broad-shouldered, with a determined jawline. Ruggedly handsome, she found herself thinking. Mid to late thirties, like her. Maybe even early forties, but he wore his skin and features well, not like some of the other Icelanders around, who seemed more weathered than the mountains.

He was blocking the snowdrifts now, stepping up to her in bulky snow pants and a heavy jacket, his hair shaggy and unruly, sticking out in all directions from under his woollen hat. He stopped in front of her, not too close, but close enough that she could feel the intensity radiating off him.

'I'm Gunnar,' he said, pulling off his gloves. 'You must be Mahlia.' He studied her face for a moment in silence, sizing her up. 'You look just like they described you.'

Mahlia was amused, even as his eyes bored into her, unsettling something deep in her belly. How had they described her? A Kiwi girl? A fragile, five-foot-five half-Maori woman, completely in over her head?

'That's right,' she said, picturing the first time Javid had looked at her like this. If only she'd known back then to run a mile. 'I'm a rescue paramedic. I've been here a month already. Good of you to join us.'

He huffed a laugh. 'I go where I'm needed.' His hand was big and strong and heat emanated straight from his palm right into her own. 'It sounds like you must have something special,' he said, cutting through the snow with her to the hut and opening the door for her.

His words made Maliah smile; she wasn't used to such compliments. Then he spoilt it.

'But you look tired,' he added. 'When was the last time you slept?'

She bristled. If there was one thing that annoyed her most it was people thinking she wasn't up to the job for any reason. 'We're all tired. But we go where we're needed,' she said, mimicking his earlier words. He bit back a smile, which seemed to settle something between them and send her heart flapping at the same time.

He pulled the creaking door shut behind them, shutting out the snow-covered mountains as well as her reply, then walked to the table, shaking off his jacket to a chorus of, 'Gunnar Johansson!' and 'Gunnar, my man!'

Everyone seemed to know him. Some jumped up from their seats, enthusiastically shaking his hand, and he reached out to them with a nod here, a friendly smile there. Some were old friends, no doubt. The women all threw their arms around him. Several seemed to hold on just a little longer than necessary. There were a couple of guys, though, in the far corner, who were frowning now, throwing each other knowing looks, nodding his way and huddling in to talk about him.

Her instincts were primed. They didn't like Gunnar. Why?

She watched him and Erik hunch over the map he'd pulled out, their fingers tracing circles. The outermost ring followed natural boundaries—a river, a mountain ridge, a coffee-coloured lake. They'd been methodically erasing possible scenarios from the list all day. Gunnar caught her eye again across the table and Maliah's heart lodged tight in her throat. Something about him made her feel simultaneously excited and cautious at the same time.

Someone had said earlier that he was a big deal, or his family were a big deal in Iceland— not that she'd been listening, really, and she hadn't the time to look him up. He was a trained renal specialist and surgeon. And he was taking some time off, like he did every year, to volunteer on the search and rescue teams.

Her radio flickered to life. Someone with a drone had just spotted an orange item of clothing, out by one of the lakes.

'We should get going,' she heard herself saying, just as Erik said the same thing in unison.

Her crew were already on their feet.

* * *

Maliah saw it first. The orange crumpled heap of something that looked a lot like a jacket tangled in the branches that swept the ground. 'Someone's here!'

'I see it,' Sven said, steering them back towards it.

The lake was iced over, a sheet of white, thanks to the fresh snow from the storm. From up here in the helicopter, the fjords held the look of giant serrated teeth around the perimeter. The iced-over craggy tops of the mountains on the horizon told her just how stranded they'd be without each other. Helpless. Like the people they were looking for.

Having flown in from New Zealand, she was only in her third week of the four-month contract she'd taken with this SAR team, but already Erik, Ásta and Sven were her family by proxy—the ones she had to rely on, day in, day out. As for Gunnar, she thought, shooting him a glance. Time would tell.

'I think I can land here,' Sven called back now.

His words were barely audible over the din of the helicopter's engines and rotors, but Gunnar was beside her in a second, his face pressed to the window, assessing the situation. Erik and Ásta checked the terrain through the opposite windows.

The trees below were sparse, a few broken stumps poking up through the snow. It was impossible to tell if it was a person's jacket from here or not, now that she thought about it.

'Hang in there,' she said under her breath to the people who were lost out here somewhere. One of the Swedish tourists had been wearing an orange jacket—they all knew it.

'Sven's a pro, in case you hadn't noticed,' Gunnar said, sensing her concern. 'I've known him since school—he wouldn't put anyone in danger.'

'It's not his flying I'm worried about,' she replied, but her cheeks grew hot at the way he was looking at her, closer than close. He smiled as the chopper lowered to the ground. His teeth were slightly jagged at the edges, milky white, still baby-like in their perfection.

'You're a tough one, aren't you?' he observed in his thick Icelandic accent.

'Is that a compliment?' she shot back, and one thick blond eyebrow shot up to his hat.

He sounded slightly American, despite his accent. She was about to ask him where exactly he was from when Sven slid the chopper almost to a stop and Gunnar sprang into action, opening the door before they were even completely stationary.

Her eyes traced his movements as he skidded down a bank and onto the frozen lake, motioning at them all to stay where they were for now. She watched from the open door with her heart in her mouth as he picked his way carefully across the ice. He crouched where the fuzzy fir trees began and started to carefully remove snow from around the object with one hand, clutching a branch with the other.

'It's a coat,' he called back to them, and her heart skidded at the confirmation.

In seconds she was on the ground, crunching over the heavy snow in her boots towards the base of the bushy tree.

'There's no one here,' he said grimly.

'Are you sure? I'll help you dig.' This was her job—to make absolutely certain there was no one here who needed their help before turning back.

She slipped, and Gunnar lunged forward with gloved hands outstretched.

'I'm fine,' she insisted, swerving his grip.

He didn't look too sure. But when he saw she wouldn't relent, a determined fire lit his ice-blue eyes and he reached out, wrapping his gloved hands around her elbows. He drew her close to him on the ice, till their faces were only inches apart.

'Careful. One wrong movement out here, one slip-up. is all it takes...'

'I know,' she interjected, taking in the severity etched in his ice-blue gaze. 'You don't have to tell me that! I've done this before in New Zealand, remember?'

His face softened and he nodded at her, amusement flickering on his mouth for just a second. 'OK, then. Sorry.'

His voice was deep and strong, his speech measured and in control, but there was a hint of gravel in there, like a trapped cough, as if he'd been screaming and had only just stopped. What was his deal? she wondered. He seemed pretty protective of her, and he barely knew her. She knew nothing about him at all, but suddenly she wanted to.

Together, they continued to remove the snow from around the coat but, just as he'd said, there was no one with it. Gunnar stood up and took off his hat, running a hand through his hair. Mahlia watched him silently from her haunches, feeling the disappointment settle in her own chest. Maybe they'd just been too late.

'We're running out of time,' she heard herself mutter. Exhaustion was seeping through her bones now.

He fixed her with an understanding gaze. 'We won't give up. We'll keep searching, no matter how long it takes. We won't abandon them.'

His voice resounded with utter conviction and it threw her, then sent her heart into a spin. Erik and Ásta were on the edge of the ice now, zipping up thick, padded parkas.

'We'll split up,' Gunnar said firmly. 'Mahlia, you and I will take that ridge over there. Erik and Ásta will take this one here.' He gestured to an icy slope. 'That way we can cover more ground, faster.'

Mahlia turned to the sky. It was difficult for an outsider to understand how swiftly the weather in Iceland could take a turn for the worse, but she'd grown pretty used to it over the last few weeks.

Even when Sven radioed in from the chopper, saying, 'Don't go too far, guys…' Gunnar didn't look fazed at all. He was already striding purposefully across the frozen lake.

Mahlia hurried after him. The snow crunched beneath Gunnar's boots ahead of her as he made his way slowly and carefully towards the trees at the other side of the lake. Mahlia watched his eyes scanning his surroundings like a hawk, matching his stride as best she could, aware of the distance between them and the chopper. That was how far they'd have to carry someone injured back to safety, if they were lucky enough to find anyone alive.

Suddenly he stopped and crouched down, motioning her over with a wave of his hand. 'Here!'

'What is it?'

Cautiously, Mahlia made her way towards

him, till she got close enough to see what he'd spotted: fresh footprints in the snow, leading away from where they were standing.

New hope and excitement surged through her. 'You don't think…?'

'Maybe they made their way out here from some hiding place, and headed back again when the storm hit,' he said, whipping out a flashlight. Technically, it was daytime. But now, in mid-March, after a storm, they needed all the help they could get.

Together, they traced the footsteps, slowly heading deeper into dense, dark forest. The crackle of fallen leaves and twigs crunched underfoot now, and Gunnar made sure to keep her slightly behind him at all times, like a bear watching out for its cub. This whole over-protection thing would have annoyed her usually, but out here, coming from him… It was weird, but she actually felt comforted by it.

'We shouldn't go too far,' she warned him, her eyes darting around vigilantly.

The air felt brittle and cold, and the wind whistling through the trees sounded a little too much like voices. This was like New Plymouth in some ways, but in so many others completely different. Alien. Full of elves, trolls and fairies, apparently, always watching. She was almost starting to think the lady from the homestead back in Reykjavik might have been onto something with all the fantastical stories she'd pretended to believe. Mount Taranaki was famous, and was swarmed with visitors in New Zealand, so picture-perfect it barely looked real. But it was more than something pretty to the Maori people; it was an ancestor…a living thing. No one was even allowed to climb to the very top.

She almost wanted to turn back, suddenly fearing the Icelandic tales might be real, but something about Gunnar's steadfast demeanour kept her going. This man was clearly a force to be reckoned with; she was safe with him. Whoever he was. She'd known him less than an hour and here she was, alone with him in an Icelandic fjord. Javid would have a fit.

She caught herself. Javid's feelings were not her concern—not any more. No more manipulation, no more sly asides or cutting passive-aggressive remarks. No more gaslighting. He was probably going out of his mind now that his control over her had been broken for good. She was just wondering what might have happened to her wedding ring after she'd slid it into an envelope and pushed it through his letterbox on her way to the airport—the bravest thing she'd ever done!—when Gunnar stuck a hand out behind him to stop her. She almost slammed into his back.

A small hut was visible just ahead, tucked

away amongst the trees. The footprints cut through the snow, heading towards it, and Gunnar picked up his pace. Mahlia held her breath as he eased open the creaking door and followed him cautiously into the cabin, her eyes adjusting to the darkness.

'Look,' she whispered, touching his arm as her heart leapt to her throat.

She could just make out a shape in the corner. A person. Moving closer, she could tell the figure was a man, lying on his side. He wasn't moving, covered in dirty blankets that he must have salvaged from this tiny abandoned squat. The remains of a burnt-out fire sat charred and black in the hearth.

'He's alive, but injured,' Gunnar said, pulling out his radio.

He spoke to Erik while Mahlia knelt down beside the man, gently touching his shoulder as she spoke softly, so as not to alarm him. 'Are you OK? Can you tell us what happened?'

No response. Mahlia shuffled out of her backpack. She could see the extent of the injuries now—scrapes along his neck, cuts on his forehead and beneath a rolled-up trouser leg, and one of his ankles was swollen to twice its size.

'Can you move?' she asked him.

He was stirring now, unable to do more than emit a pained groan. Taking off his coat, Gunnar carefully wrapped it around him and offered his hand for support as the man attempted to push himself up into a seated position. Together, they managed to sit him upright, but he winced in agony when they tried to move his arm.

Mahlia assessed his wounds, trying not to focus on how cold she was. She unzipped her backpack and pulled out the necessary supplies: sterile cotton swabs, antiseptic solution, gauze pads and bandages. Gently she cleaned his wounds, taking care not to cause him any further discomfort, feeling Gunnar's eyes on her the whole time.

Outside the wind was howling again, bending trees at its whim, their branches and leaves crackling like fireworks.

Sven was radioing in. 'Hurry up, guys. Get back here as fast as you can. The weather's turning.'

The man's skin was cold and clammy to the touch, but thankfully his pulse was steady and strong. Mahlia wrapped a bandage around his neck wound. She would have to treat the gashes on his head in the chopper. Gunnar helped support him as she moved to address his injured ankle.

'It's not broken, but it could be dislocated,' she told him.

'Erik's on his way across the lake,' he replied,

helping her wrap a tight elastic bandage around the man's ankle for support.

This was definitely the pilot; he matched the description they had of him. But where were the Swedish couple who'd been in the plane with him? Where was the plane? All this would have to be resolved, but for now all they could do was get this guy back to the chopper as fast as they could.

Mahlia slung his arm around her neck and asked him to put his weight on her, while Gunnar held him up from the other side. 'This is probably going to hurt,' she warned him. 'But we need to get you mobile. The chopper's not far.'

The pilot winced in pain, but with their support he was able to stand. His breath was laboured and heavy as slowly they made their way from the cabin, back out through the snow and across the lake where, to her relief, Erik and Ásta were ready to help him back to the helicopter.

'No sign of the others?' Erik asked hopefully, as he and Gunnar lifted the man inside.

Mahlia felt ill with worry. The two Swedish tourists couldn't have gone far, if the orange jacket was indeed a sign that at least one of them was around somewhere, but the snow was picking up again now. They had no choice but to abandon this location for the meantime and get the chopper out to a safe location, where their injured pilot could be transported to Reykjavik.

'We did all we could,' Gunnar told her, as the air turned grey around them and the rotors churned like a machine gun above. Soon they were flying blind through a haze of snow, but thankfully Erik was the pro that Gunnar had told him he was, and all that mattered now was getting the man to safety.

Mahlia pressed her lips together; she was soaking wet and freezing. 'But maybe we overlooked something, guys. The other two are still out there.'

'We'll find them,' said Gunnar, fixing his blue eyes on hers, making her pulse quicken. 'Someone will find them.'

She watched his lips, waiting for a word like *eventually*, or two words like *dead or alive*. He seemed to know without her saying that she didn't think they'd find the others alive, because he folded his arms and shook his head wryly, even before Ásta spoke.

'Miracles do happen out here sometimes. We can never stop hoping for them, anyway.'

'We'll start again in the morning,' Erik said. 'First thing. We all need sleep,' he added, before turning directly to her. 'Mahlia, you've been on your feet since six a.m.'

The look in his kind eyes moved her. Gunnar,

who'd stayed quiet, fixed his concerned gaze on her again. Suddenly it mattered what he thought of her.

'I'm used to being tired,' she said, to Gunnar, not Erik. 'I'm fine.'

Then she turned back to the pilot, who was slipping in and out of consciousness with hypothermia. It was taking every last ounce of her energy to stay awake in the biting cold.

When they touched down at the hangar just outside of Reykjavik, the bitter wind whirled snow into her eyes and she felt her eyelids droop, even as the doors sprang open on the waiting ambulance. The medics rushed out to assist with transferring the pilot onto a stretcher, and she watched as they ushered him into their care.

Gunnar was pacing the ground, talking on the phone. Sven, Erik and Ásta said their goodbyes and piled into a Jeep together. Mahlia made for her own vehicle, thankful yet again for the snow chains on the tyres. Sleep was all she wanted now. Sweet, beautiful sleep.

'Hey, would you mind giving me a ride?' Gunnar asked suddenly, hurrying up behind her now, shoving his phone back into his pocket.

The presence of his bulk behind her sent a tingle down her spine. He gestured to the pockets of his snow pants, now pulled inside out. Then he pointed to his SUV, alone in the car park, slowly gathering another layer of thick white snow.

'I must have lost my keys somewhere on the lake,' he said. 'I have spares back at my place.'

Mahlia sucked in a quiet breath, realising how gorgeous he actually was up close, even if she couldn't really read him most of the time. Well, maybe if she drove him home she'd find out more?

CHAPTER TWO

THEY RODE IN SILENCE, the heater on full blast and the car filling with hot air that only intensified her exhaustion and the sting of her lips. Mahlia felt as if she was looking at everything through a foggy lens, but she had to stay awake. She still had to email the solicitor about the divorce papers, which Javid was still refusing to sign.

She kept biting her chafed lips, feeling the roughness of them against her teeth and with her tongue. Eventually the silence got a little awkward.

'So…' they started at the same time.

Gunnar grunted a laugh, catching her eyes in the mirror. The sound made her pulse quicken even more than it had earlier, when he'd looked at her as if…as if he admired her.

'So, Mahlia. What do you do all day when you're not on a search and rescue call?'

'You mean back in New Plymouth, where I'm from? I'm a paramedic there too, but I'm contracted here for a few months. I'm kind of exploring another idea too, actually.'

She paused. There was hardly any point in telling him she was trying to get as far away from her controlling ex-husband as possible—that she'd left him six weeks ago, still begging her to take him back.

'I'm a mountain biker,' she continued.

He nodded with interest.

'And I'm in the process of developing a new e-bike for the market. It has an electric motor, and various danger-detection capabilities, so it'll help get people with mobility difficulties out and about more on all kinds of terrain.'

Gunnar turned to her, his attention focused fully on her face now. He listened, studying her eyes and her face as she spoke, and she found herself inserting more passion into her tone with each sentence, like she always did, without thinking, when she started on this topic.

She told him how she was meeting soon with Inka, who was a wheelchair user and the programme analyst here at the Icelandic Wilderness Association. In a similar mission to the one Mahlia had started in Egmont National Park, she was keen to gather updated data on various wilderness trails to determine their safety. Together with Inka, she hoped to combine her mission with locating the best places for the bike to be trialled and enjoyed by users.

Gunnar smiled warmly, running a hand through his hair, sending it spiking up even more. Adorable... 'My brother Demus has multiple sclerosis,' he said. 'I've always wished there was a way to give him his freedom back. He used to ride motorcycles with me all over the place when I lived in the US.'

'Then he's exactly the kind of person I want to help,' she said, tucking away the information that Gunnar had used to live in America. 'My bike can be used by both able-bodied individuals *and* people with a physical disability. It's specifically designed to be adaptive, so you can customise it to your ability level. A good friend of mine at home was paralysed from the waist down a few years ago.' She paused, picturing Jessica, hooked up to all those machines after her accident. 'She was told she'd never cycle again, but she wasn't going to let anyone's opinion hold her back. She was the one who inspired me to do something to help, so we could ride together again someday.'

Gunnar was looking at her with such interest now, even as he answered his chiming phone. Pride swelled her heart. A new feeling, she noted. Javid had always hated hearing anything about her side project.

Gunnar spoke in Icelandic as she chewed her

lips. Damn, she needed a tube of lip salve so badly. She'd meant to buy one yesterday, but with everything going on with the search she'd clean run out of time.

'Listen, that was Erik, calling about the pilot...' Gunnar said when he'd hung up.

'Yes?'

He paused a moment. His face was too grave now for her liking and her heart bucked.

'He has severe hypothermia, but the doctors say he'll survive. He's heavily medicated and they're going to keep him sedated. He did mention the Swedish couple, though.'

She nodded, feeling her hands ball into fists on the steering wheel.

'It's not good news. The plane went down in the lake. The pilot got out through the window. When he came up it was already sinking. The divers will go down first thing in the morning for the...for them.'

A rush of nausea flooded her veins as she pictured the scene: those poor people, trying to get out, realising all hope was lost. The orange jacket must have floated out of the lake. Maybe the pilot had left it as a sign for them to look for him there. Maybe he'd already known then that he'd be the only survivor.

Gunnar's gaze was on her again. 'Sorry,' she

said quickly, realising her eyes were wet. 'I don't usually get emotional, but…'

'You haven't slept. It happens…it's OK.' His voice was still measured, but his words were coated with kindness now. 'I'm sorry, Mahlia.'

'It's not your fault,' she replied, swallowing down her emotions, realising he hadn't bought her previous claim that she wasn't tired at all.

He swept a hand across his jaw. 'Take the next right.'

'Which hotel are you?' she asked, doing as he asked, hitting a right through a flurry of snow till the modern Hallgrimskirkja cathedral with all its organ key angles came into view in the headlights.

The streets were empty. The grey skies and snow seemed to smother the city, and the crowds of tourists who usually flooded this area had been left with nowhere else to go but home.

'I have a place here,' he said, simply. 'Just here—pull over.'

She did as he asked, just as her phone rang from its place in its holder on the dash. *Javid.* She grimaced, flicking it to silent.

'You're not going to answer that?' he asked.

She shook her head, embarrassed, noting the modern apartment building, the copper and glass encased in a gleaming stone wall, the dragon pillar with its mouth open, holding a lamp to light the steps. His place. This looked like a very expensive place to live—not that anything in Reykjavik was cheap. He obviously earned good money as a surgeon, but she remembered now something about his family being in banking.

He opened the door, but hesitated, turning back to her again, eyes narrowed as they studied her mouth in a way that made her stomach flip. 'Wait here.'

She gaped in response as he slammed the door shut and sprinted up the steps to the entranceway. Tapping her nails on the steering wheel, she yawned, and ignored Javid's second call—why would he not stop calling her? Wasn't leaving him for Iceland enough to drum it home that she was gone from his life for good?

What was Gunnar doing? Who was Gunnar Johansson, even? If she weren't so damn tired and shaken she'd ask him all kinds of things. But all she wanted to do now was sleep.

Suddenly he was back. 'Here.'

In a whirl of snowflakes that rushed in with his hand he deposited a small cylindrical tube into her palm. 'Get some rest,' he instructed, before she could respond. 'I'll see you soon. We're on the same team now.'

'I guess we are,' she said, looking away, wishing her heart would stop making her all doe-eyed over him. 'But aren't you due back in surgery? I heard you're a renal specialist?'

'I oversee Iceland's only kidney transplant pro-gramme for most of the year,' he said matter-of-factly, with no trace of ego. 'November through April is the best time to take my break. More people need me out here on the search teams.'

A real hero, she thought, impressed.

'Wait,' she said, before he could shut the door again. 'I'll see you tomorrow, right? I'm still coming. Just in case...'

'Just in case we *do* find them alive?' He frowned.

'Just in case,' she repeated, as firmly as she could. It didn't seem right to just give up. 'I'll tell Erik when he calls me.'

He held her eyes a moment, sizing her up again in a way that made her nervous. Then he bobbed his head and shut the door again.

Mahlia stared at the object in her hand. A brand-new, unopened tube of lip salve. Cherry-flavoured, no less. With relief, she applied it to her lips in the mirror, feeling the soothing balm calm her instantly. How had he known? Did she really look that terrible? Or, more to the point, had he been looking at her lips long enough to notice that she needed this?

The tiny dead creature in her stomach fluttered back to life—the one that Javid had stomped on again and again. Her ex had done his best to convince her that all her friends were bad for her; that she most certainly did not need to speak to a therapist about her spiralling lack of self-worth whenever she was with him; that she did drink too much on company nights out; that she didn't need to work as hard as she did because it made him look like a miserly provider. And every single time he'd told her any or all those things another part of her had shrivelled up and died.

Now, though…

A light flicked on in the apartment two floors up as she pulled away. Glancing in her mirrors, she swore she saw Gunnar in the window, watching her go.

Gunnar was right, of course. There were no more survivors.

Mahlia watched the last of the scuba divers surface from her place in the helicopter. The wind howled like a banshee wail, stealing words from her freezing cold lips and blasting them away as Gunnar was lowered from the chopper towards the ice, swinging on the winch like a tiny figure in a giant snow globe.

His orange jumpsuit was the brightest thing for miles, a beacon against the grey-white tundra as he touched down on the life raft on the

BECKY WICKS 35

frozen lake. The divers had set it up in case the ice broke and took the crew down, too.

She held her breath next to Ásta as Gunnar set about bringing the two Swedish tourists up through a carefully cut hole in the ice, and she kept her eyes on him, watching him master the buckles and straps and clips and harnesses, all while the weather did everything in its power to halt his expert mission.

She found herself concerned for him, even though he clearly knew what he was doing. This was her team, her crew, and she'd held out hope till the break of dawn, till arriving here back at the lake, that things would turn out differently. But she'd also been thinking about Gunnar, specifically. And about what she'd learned about him this morning on the Internet, at five a.m. over coffee.

She couldn't help feeling a little sorry for him now.

Gunnar's father, Ingólfur Johansson, had spent five years incarcerated in Kviabryggja Prison. after some privately owned commercial banks had defaulted. Ingólfur, Fjallabanki Bank's former chief executive officer, had been convicted of market manipulation and fraud and, from what she'd been able to gather online, a lot of people in this very small country had turned against Gunnar's whole family because of it.

She watched Gunnar now, on his ascent with one of the bodies. It was hard to look, knowing that someone in that thick black bag had set out for a day of excitement and adventure and wound up like this. She'd been on search and rescue teams on and off around her work for years, but if she was quite honest not even New Zealand's harshest winter could have prepared her for this.

'The ambulance will meet us at the road when we've finished here,' Erik told them, readying himself to help Gunnar, who was still swaying perilously on his steel wire, navigating the way towards them slowly but surely with his load.

She cleared the last of the room in the chopper for the unfortunate victims while her heart roared in her chest, almost louder than the rotors.

A little later Mahlia found herself watching Gunnar talking to Erik and the police as she waited for them, sipping on a much-needed coffee. The hangar was still a foot deep in snow outside, despite the shovelled snowdrifts to the sides. All the cops here had guns on show, she mused, rubbing her eyes. They were all exceptionally good-looking, too.

She pictured Javid, the night he'd dressed up as a policeman for Halloween. It must have been two years into their seven-year marriage. He'd put in as little effort as possible and had berated her for having too much of herself on display in her Cat Woman costume. He'd forced her to leave early with him. That was the same night he'd told her to give up on the adapted e-bikes project, that it would never go anywhere. It had only been a flicker of an idea at the time. She'd continued with it largely to prove him wrong.

Did he miss her? Or was he calling her incessantly to remind her that he didn't need her in his life? It still made her anxious, remembering how she'd finally told him it was over, face to face in the park, right after he'd told her she needed to walk straighter or she'd have a hunchback by the time she was forty-five. Something had snapped then. Years of his catty, snarky comments, made without a trace of humour, had all suddenly come to a head. She'd ditched him right by a gang of burly motorcyclists, all of them bigger than him, so he wouldn't dare go after her.

'You know, I don't think I did,' Ásta said suddenly.

Ásta was a tall, fierce-looking native Icelander with a background as coach of Iceland's all-women rugby team, but now she was wondering out loud if she'd fed her cat Twinkie that morning, what with her husband still being in the hospital.

'Hmmm…' Mahlia responded, distracted.

Gunnar caught her eye from across the road.

He was still in the orange jumpsuit, looking the sexiest anyone had ever looked in a jumpsuit, no question. His hair was as sticky-outy as yesterday, the opposite to Javid's closely shaven stubble. It had always felt a little like sandpaper to her...

She dragged her stare away quickly, forcing her mind to get back to where she needed it. She was psyching herself up to go home, to her rental apartment, and get on with her presentation for Inka. Working on the e-bike trial with some keen, physically challenged participants they'd sourced together would hopefully take her mind off the sight of those body bags...and Javid.

Funny, though, how her persistent mind kept going back to Gunnar, and what his father had done. It hadn't really felt right to probe the Internet for too much information on his past, but just finding out what little she had about his family made her heart go out to him. Iceland was a place where everyone knew *everyone*, and everyone's business too. Suddenly the looks on those men's faces last night in the community centre made much more sense.

All those years ago market manipulation and fraud had had a domino effect on the entire country, and on the way everyone outside it had viewed Iceland back then, too. She'd been twenty, so Gunnar had probably been only a few years older than that when his father had been held accountable and stripped of his ill-gotten gains. Gunnar's life must have been only just beginning when everyone had turned against his family. She'd read about his parents' divorce, too. Kaðlín Johansson had been an iconic TV news anchor when it had happened, and now… she wasn't.

The prison in western Iceland where his father had spent time looked awful! It stood alone on a windswept cape overlooked by a dormant volcano. It looked like a hellscape to her, surrounded on one side by the hostile North Atlantic and snow-covered lava rock on the other. Had Gunnar ever visited his father there during his sentence? she wondered. Or was that when he'd moved to the US?

'Earth to Mahlia?'

Ásta waved a hand across her face, just missing her nose. Ugh, she'd zoned out again, thinking about Gunnar! Why did his life suddenly seem more interesting than anything else she had going on in her own? *Focus!*

Erik and Gunnar were striding purposefully towards them, and the sight was shooting adrenaline through her again.

'I think something must have happened. I guess Twinkie's going to have to wait for her food a little longer.'

Sure enough, Erik's radio was buzzing. 'Road accident out on the Svalvogavegur. We'll go ahead in my car,' he said to Ásta, who sprang into action.

'Mahlia will follow in the search and rescue truck, with me,' Gunnar added.

Her heart leapt at the sound of her name coming from his mouth, gruff, but loaded with purpose that somehow made her feel extra special and essential to the mission. She was used to feeling unseen and unheard in Javid's company, so this was new. And why was he so keen to have her with him? Had he been thinking about her too? She kind of hoped he had…

He met her eyes as he scrunched up his paper coffee cup in one hand and tossed it into a trash can. 'I'd let you drive, but this is a dangerous road, and if the weather changes it's not a great place to be behind the wheel.'

No point arguing with that. 'Then let's go.'

She scrunched up her own cup with new determination, tossed it hard, and missed the trash can by a mile. Hurriedly she picked it up, placed it into the trash can carefully, and followed him.

He smirked at her as she slid into the passenger seat of the sturdy truck, loaded with all the supplies and equipment they might need on land. 'Basketball not your thing?'

'Very funny,' she said, clicking on her seatbelt as heat rushed to her cheeks and made her blood race.

Gunnar drove them quickly but steadily behind Erik's vehicle along the winding road. He reassured her on the way, talking about the top-mounted floodlight system and the twelve-thousand-pound front-mounted winch—which, to be fair, no one had bothered explaining to her until now. He knew his stuff. Which was comforting and also hot.

Despite her guilt for knowing more about him than she should at this point, she found herself wondering even more about Gunnar Johansson—like how long he'd watched her car from his window last night, and whether he'd noticed yet how her lips were much better.

CHAPTER THREE

THE ACCIDENT SCENE was a mess. The cops who'd called Erik were already on site as Mahlia sprang from the truck. She assessed the black skid marks on the road, the debris strewn everywhere—broken glass, frayed wires and pieces of metal that had clearly used to be various parts of a motorcycle. Then she saw the rider.

Rushing over, she knelt on the freezing ground in her padded snow trousers. A man in his mid-twenties sat on the snow-covered roadside, cradling his head in his hands, dressed in torn leathers. His helmet was cracked beside him on the ground—a reminder of what might have befallen his skull if he hadn't been wearing it. Miraculously he didn't look too hurt, but there was blood on his left knee, seeping through the leather.

'This is Arni Sturlson. He swerved to avoid a car,' one of the policemen told her, coming up behind her with Erik.

'Where's the car?' she asked, pulling out

gauze and antiseptics and making a tourniquet for the man's leg. All she could see were black lava fields on one side and trees on the other.

'I heard them shouting for help,' the motorcyclist told her, wincing in pain as she snipped at his leathers some more. 'They're alive down there.'

'Who was shouting?' She kept calm as she hurried to curb the bleeding.

Gunnar raced past in a blur of orange, and suddenly she knew what Arni meant…why they'd been called as the closest emergency crew.

Gunnar had stopped at the edge of the road. Another cop was pointing downwards, craning his neck to see down deep into the ravine.

'Wait here and try not to move. The ambulance is coming,' she told Arni now.

She rushed over to Gunnar, but his arm came out to block her. 'Careful!'

Her heart wedged in her throat as she peered over his arm and over the edge. It was pretty far down, but she could just make out a shape—the car.

Somehow Arni Sturlson had managed to save himself by swerving in time, preventing an unquestionable tragedy, but the SUV had tumbled head-over-heels, down at least twenty metres. It was perched between the jagged rocks below like a shiny metallic bird's nest.

'It's still in one piece,' Gunnar said incredulously, as Ásta ran over with an armful of climbing ropes.

Erik paused on the radio as not one, but two voices sounded out from the vehicle below.

Mahlia clutched Gunnar's arm. A chill ran down her spine. 'There's a child down there!'

'We need an anchor. Help me tie this round that tree,' he said to her, new urgency coating his words as he took the climbing ropes and hurried to a thick tree nearby.

Snow sprayed from its branches the second it was disturbed, coating their shoulders as they secured the line. The wind had died down, thankfully. It was at least a little easier to do everything when the snow and wind weren't lashing at their faces.

Gunnar made quick work of threading the rope from the tree through the rappel rings and attaching them to his waist. 'Get the stretchers ready,' he told her. 'I don't know what I'm bringing up.'

Several other trees along the ledge had been flattened, no doubt by the car. They'd probably slowed its descent somewhat, she thought as Erik took over, installing the rappel back-up, then guiding Gunnar's descent down the steep, rocky cliff.

She held her breath as he moved, watching the top of his helmet, praying no rocks or broken branches would land on him. The bulk of him as he descended, kicking at the rocks as he went in heavy boots, sent snow, ice, leaves and shards of jagged rocks splintering off the vertical surface in his wake. Some bounced off the car below.

Mahlia heard the child scream again, and she winced as she dragged the stretchers from the rescue vehicle.

It was hard to comprehend how anyone could survive such an accident and yet here they were: mother and eleven-year-old daughter, bruised, sore but alive.

'I thought we were going to die down there.' The woman sniffed as Mahlia took the pale little girl's vitals where she lay on a stretcher under a quickly darkening sky.

Kitta Guðmundsson had been driving carefully north towards her mother's house in the next village when the speeding motorcyclist had taken her by surprise on a blind corner. He was vocal in his apologies, although the police weren't letting him off the hook. Mahlia listened as they questioned him and gave him a stern talking-to about speeding.

By the time she'd run her checks on the little girl, and Gunnar and Erik had navigated removing the car efficiently from the crop of trees with the lauded front-mounted winch, a road assistance vehicle had appeared to clear the debris from the road. And by the time all three injured but lucky people had been deposited at the hospital for further check-ups, and the rescue team were back at the hangar base, the darkness had closed in on Reykjavik and Mahlia had only just stopped shaking with adrenaline.

What a day.

'I have to go and check on my cat,' Ásta announced. Then she stopped halfway to her car, wincing to herself. 'I should probably go to the hospital first and see my husband.'

'I'll come and see how he's doing, too,' Erik said. The two of them left in their respective vehicles, leaving her and Gunnar alone. Again.

Before she could announce her plan to stop her growling stomach by pouncing like a snow cat onto the first morsel of food she came across in her pathetically stocked fridge, Gunnar cleared his throat behind her.

'Did you lose your keys again?' She smiled, turning to find him leaning against his car, a beacon of orange in the floodlights.

The sight of his wild, unruly hair and sharp jawline, illuminated by the glow of the floodlight behind her, did funny things to her insides. He dangled a keychain on one finger.

'No,' he said. 'But I forgot to eat all day and I owe you for last night. Do you have any plans for dinner?'

* * *

Mahlia could hardly believe it when they pulled up at the famous Blue Lagoon. Milky blue water surrounded the modern wooden structure, turning it into a fairy-tale fortress in the floodlights. Behind them the mountaintops shone white on a rare clear night. People came here to swim in the healing, steaming waters, but Gunnar had brought her to the restaurant.

She'd read that it was one of the most expensive in Iceland, which made her wonder if he still had access to a hidden stash of that dirty money his father had allegedly been stripped of. Surely not... She didn't want to even think these things...or be so attracted to him when she had come here to avoid a man who'd showered so much attention on her she'd suffocated. But how could she not?

The concierge took their coats. She pressed her hands to the front of her wraparound dress and hoped she looked OK in it, with her black boots and sheer tights, as they were guided quickly and politely up two staircases into the show-stopping restaurant.

When he'd dropped her home to change, saying he'd be back for her in one hour, she'd tried on every single item in her wardrobe twice. Trusting a man she'd only just met to take her anywhere was new to her, but there was some-

thing about this man that was hard to put a finger on. Normally she'd have made her excuses
and gone home to be alone, where no man could
twist her thoughts the way Javid had a habit of
doing even now! But Gunnar and all his mys-
teries had her mind spinning and, to be honest,
any time that wasn't spent worrying about Javid
flying over here to find her was time well spent.

'A friend of mine is doing a guest chef and
wine pairing thing—I promised him ages ago
I'd come,' Gunnar had told her in the car, by way
of explanation.

Now, sitting opposite him at a table with the
most impressive view of Iceland she had ever
seen, she was struggling to tell herself this was
a normal night out. He'd calmed his hair and put
on a pale blue shirt that matched his eyes—an
expensive one, she noted. The buttons were en-
graved with something she couldn't read, and the
cuffs were turned up, revealing a Rolex watch
and more of his big, strong hands than she'd ever
seen before. He'd always worn gloves. The sight
of them made her instantly picture them on her
body...

'I thought we'd go to a restaurant in Reykjavik,' she told him, suddenly self-conscious as
a waiter fussed over them, placing a soft cloth
napkin in her lap. They'd driven half an hour to
get here.

'Is this place OK for you?' he asked her now, pressing his hands together in a steeple as the waiter placed a wine list down in front of him.

Oops, had she offended him?

'It's fine—how's the shark here?'

'It's actually pretty good, with a few potatoes and...'

'I'll be fine with the salmon,' she said hurriedly.

His eyes were glinting in the candlelight now, mischievous and teasing, and the spicy scent of his aftershave with its hint of manly musk was as bewitching at the views. This was so unlike her... To be rendered a teenager again. To be looked at like this—as if she was a woman with worth and merit, and not an inconvenience.

When he'd ordered the wine, the chef came over to greet him. The two men chatted briefly in Icelandic, and she noticed several people at a table further along throwing speculative glances his way. They didn't look at all impressed that he was here, and were clearly still chattering amongst themselves about him when the chef left.

'I've known that guy for years; he's a great chef,' Gunnar told her, as she took an awkward sip of her crisp, cold Sauvignon Blanc, glancing over her glass.

Gunnar noticed her discomfort. He glanced

around, catching the people looking. Instantly the expression on his face resembled a storm.

'Those people don't seem to want us here,' she whispered.

'That would be the Johansson reputation at work. I try to ignore it. There's not much else I can do. Do you want to leave?'

Something in his tone tore at her heart. She'd wanted to leave every place Javid had taken her, but now... 'No, I don't want to leave. It's because of the bank and your father, right? I heard some...stuff.'

Gunnar took a swig from his crystal wine glass, forcing a smile to his face that didn't show in his eyes. 'It'd be impossible for you not to hear *stuff*. People think what they want to think about me and they don't always keep it quiet.'

It was almost as if he'd accepted his fate. She pressed her hands to the table. 'But you save lives, literally every day, so how can people hold anything against you?'

'You don't know my people,' he said grimly. 'Stubborn Viking mentality.'

A thin smile crossed his lips as he stared out of the window. The rolling glacier and snow-dusted volcanoes with their slow flowing rivers of lava made her feel as if they were on a movie set, but he didn't seem to notice to it.

The chef came back, bearing plates of the reddest salmon she'd ever seen, with pickled beets and rye bread. She nibbled in silence, feeling the tension mount.

Say something.

'So, you said you once lived in the US? Did you move there after the banks crashed? To get away from it all?'

Gunnar put his fork down. He studied her carefully, as if weighing something up, and she swallowed her salmon, feeling every last morsel slide down her throat under his blue-eyed scrutiny.

'I was already there when it all happened.'

He explained how he'd moved to California two years before the crash. He'd been twenty-two then, and had taken a scholarship at Stanford University's School of Medicine. His mother was half-American, so he'd wanted to live and work there for a while.

'Everyone told me not to come home after it happened—they said it was a nightmare. So I stayed in California, even after my...' He trailed off.

The expression on his face put her on high alert, despite his jokes. Even after his what?

'I started working for myself...got a life going that was pretty good, actually. You know, I still dream about the burgers at the diner on my block.' He dragged a hand through his hair.

'Then Demus got diagnosed with MS, six and a half years ago, and I knew it was time to come home.'

'Your brother?' she said. Why was her heart galloping like a pony?

He nodded. 'Dad left the country as soon as he was released from jail. Ma was…not in a position to help Demus. He's my older brother, my only sibling. He's pretty independent, you know, and still lives alone, luckily, but I wanted to be here for him. So, yeah, I came back permanently.'

'You must have come back to a totally different world after what happened to your dad,' she said, trying to let it sink in.

Gunnar said nothing, but the look on his face told her everything. His father's betrayal had blasted his world to pieces. No doubt his brother's diagnosis had, too.

More food appeared in front of them— steaming bowls of lobster soup—and they ate in silence again, while her mind churned with questions she shouldn't ask. This attraction to Gunnar was already highly inappropriate. She was still fending off Javid! And she was supposed to be enjoying being alone.

'So, what do you do when you're not saving lives with the search and rescue team?' she ventured anyway. 'Or what don't you do?'

She watched his mouth twitch and hoped he

didn't think she was stepping out of line, but he told her how his bouldering and climbing adventures in the US had led him to lead weekend tours in the mountains there. He'd trained as a winchman in more recent years, when he'd returned home to Iceland, and enjoyed search and rescue as much as his time in surgery.

'You live in Reykjavik full time?' she asked.

'I have a couple of places for when I need to escape the city.'

Escape. There was a word she could related to.

'Does that happen a lot?' she asked now, just as the people who'd been gossiping about him glanced in her direction. Two of them were laughing.

She stared them down till they looked away. Gunnar caught her and she flushed—it wasn't her job to defend him, so why did she feel obligated to?

'I just like to be alone,' he told her, scraping back his chair as if trying to distance himself from her suddenly.

Her brain went right to another question. Had he ever been able to have a serious relationship here, with half of the island seemingly against him?

'You say you have a couple of places?' she said instead, and he stuck a fork into lettuce heart, nodded.

Impressive, she thought. From what she knew of him, he really didn't seem to be the kind of man who'd take dirty money accumulated from the misfortune of others. He had clearly done well as a surgeon, separately from his family's former wealth.

'I have a little cabin outside of Reykjavik, about fifteen minutes up north. Or an hour if we're stuck in a blizzard. Sometimes I take my brother,' he said, putting his napkin down on the table. 'We sit up and talk, play music, watch the lights…or the midnight sun.'

Mahlia smiled as the chef delivered a fresh sorbet and a sweet white wine for dessert, picturing the cabin and the midnight sun, and in the winter the northern lights dancing above them in the wilderness. He obviously cared a great deal about his brother if he'd moved away from the States and his life there, risked everyone looking down on him and his family. in order to look out for Demus here. He really was a hero.

What was the catch?

There was always a catch; she'd just failed to see it at first with Javid.

Not that she was here to get all dreamy-eyed over a guy anyway, she reminded herself, turning her gaze out to the blue lagoon, steaming below them under the soft orange lights. Several people were floating, or standing with hot drinks and glasses of wine in the mist. The stars were the brightest she'd seen them since arriving here.

It suddenly occurred to her… Was this a date?

The notion sent her cold. The reasons she was here in Iceland were to get the new e-assist devices into trial mode somewhere other than New Zealand and learn from the SAR crew, all while staying well out of Javid's way. Hopefully with enough time and distance between them he'd finally agree to sign the damn divorce papers.

She felt her fist clench under her seat as her heartbeat sped up. If Javid so much as suspected she was on anything resembling a date he would come for her. He'd try and assert his claim over his property, or what he thought was his property, like he always did. He would get into her head. She was still too scared to actually *be* there, where he could physically reach her with all his powers of persuasion.

An alert on Gunnar's phone drew her eyes from the steaming blue lagoon and her thoughts back to him.

'Looks like we might be in luck tonight,' he said, making her heart leap even more.

What?

'The northern lights?' He turned the phone to her.

An app was open, showing circles of yellow

and swirls of neon-green. It sent alerts when the northern lights were due to put on a show.

'I know you don't have a bathing suit with you,' he said, motioning to the waiter for the bill. 'But should we rent you one?'

CHAPTER FOUR

MAHLIA FELT GOOSEBUMPS flaring beneath her fluffy white robe as Gunnar ushered her to the edge of the lagoon, his hand featherlight against the small of her back. Her nostrils quivered at the mild scent of sulphur. The stars sparkled above them in infinite constellations and for a brief moment, as she watched him slip off his robe and stride out ahead of her into the warm blue liquid and curling steam, the night sky and everything below it seemed alive with possibility.

She'd never seen anything like this before—never so much as stepped foot into a geothermal pool. Sure, they had them in New Zealand, but she'd always been too busy or, if she was totally honest with herself now, too afraid of Javid criticising her choice of swimwear. The beauty of it all was mesmerising. And Gunnar with his shirt off...

Oh, my. She had not been prepared for this at all.

The steam rose from the pool and cloaked his

form with a foggy haze as he turned back to her and beckoned her in. Only his broad shoulders and muscular arms were visible now. He looked protective which, combined with his chosen profession, told her he was someone she could instinctively trust—as long as she didn't get all goo-goo over him.

But, oh, the way his arm had been flung out to stop her at the cliff-edge earlier today...the way he'd caught her on the pond on day one. *Hot.*

Sliding off her robe, she feigned a confidence in her body that she didn't quite feel, glancing up at the restaurant windows, to where they'd just been sitting.

'Don't be scared...it's not deep,' he told her, stepping towards her again.

His eyes lingered on her as she took the ramp down from the cold concrete deck into the warm waters of the lagoon. The temperature was just right—not too hot or cold—and a welcome relief from the frigid winter air.

'Drink?' he asked her now, motioning to the open bar in the middle of the pool. 'I was going to get us a hot chocolate.'

'Sounds perfect,' she said, taking in the couples standing close, arms around each other in the water. None of these people seemed to have noticed Gunnar, and if they had they didn't care.

Mahlia felt herself relax, spreading her arms

out along the steaming surface. At the bar, Gunnar pulled himself onto a stool. His body rippled with solid muscle. His shoulders were square, his chest full and broad. His abs were so tight they looked as if they must have been carved from marble...or just honed from years of climbing rocks and boulders and working the winch.

Up close, as he'd taken off his robe back there, she'd seen the fine hair that covered his chest. It tapered to a light blond point, disappearing into the waistband of his shorts in a way that made her question her type. She'd always assumed she liked dark-haired men, like Javid. Now, everything about Javid repulsed her—so much so that she had a new type now. Blond. Gunnar-blond.

What did he think of her? she wondered, before she could tell herself it didn't matter. Javid had always said her hips were the best kind for birthing, but that her legs were too chunky to be feminine.

Screw Javid, she thought crossly. He was interfering in her life even now. This was a new start for her. Being free was imperative. She'd spent seven years bending to Javid's whims and now she was here. With *this* guy...who probably just wanted to get to know and trust his co-worker. Finding people who trusted him was obviously not all that easy for Gunnar.

'Hot chocolate?' He was back now, handing

her a cup loaded on the top with whipped cream. Emphasis on 'hot', she groaned to herself, unable to move her eyes from the lines of his glistening shoulder blades.

Stop drooling, she told herself sternly. *You are his co-worker; that's all he sees you as.*

Besides, there was no way any man was taking control of her again, physically or emotionally. No way.

Then there was a squeal. Several squeals.

'Look.' Gunnar pointed upwards, guiding her to the side of the pool so they could put their cups down.

Her gaze shifted skywards as they waded, and she couldn't help the grin that spread from ear to ear. The northern lights!

They started off weak and slow, like musical notes dancing out of sync in the silence. Then they changed their speed, starting a more enthusiastic, fully choreographed dance in vibrant greens, yellows and purples. They flickered across the dark sky like a liquid rainbow, snatching her breath away. It was so breathtakingly beautiful she found she had tears in her eyes. She'd never seen them as clear and bright as this.

'You know,' Gunnar said now, floating on his back beside her, 'when we were kids, growing up, our parents used to tell us the northern lights were monsters.'

'Monsters?'

'It was their way of making sure we went home at night before it got too late. We were so afraid of the monsters in the sky we used to run home before they could get us.'

Mahlia laughed. 'I can't believe you grew up afraid of this!'

'We literally ran away from them.' He laughed too, and his arm pressed against hers as they were swept together in the water. 'I missed them when I was in California, though.'

'You're proud of your country. I can tell.' Her fingers brushed his for just a little too long as her heart thumped behind her rented bathing suit. He was so sexy…all wet and glowing beneath the northern lights. Almost as sexy as he looked in his jumpsuit.

She would remember this night, she thought, and this new, addictive feeling of awe, power and freedom, for as long as she lived.

'I am proud of my country,' he said. 'I never stopped being proud to be Icelandic. Even if I'm not exactly proud to be my father's son.'

Mahlia turned to him. 'What your father did isn't your fault. It shouldn't be a reflection on you.'

She felt him tense beside her. He was quiet for a moment and she sensed there was a lot about her new colleague that she'd never know. He'd taken on a more than he'd bargained for, thanks to his father's actions, but none of that was Gunnar's fault.

Then he turned to her, with a different expression in his eyes. A look of shrewd perception that told her he had questions.

'What really brought you here, Mahlia? You could work on your e-bikes in plenty of rugged terrain back in New Zealand, couldn't you? You could join a search and rescue team there.'

'I like to see new places,' she said, as her stomach did somersaults.

'This seems like a long way to go from home, though, on your own.'

She forced her eyes back to the light show in the sky. He was trained to be assertive and astute, to notice the finer details. Of course he'd ask. 'I just like to be alone,' she told him tightly, mimicking what he'd said to her earlier.

He huffed a laugh. 'Touché. A fellow loner. I won't ask any more questions. All I know is that people don't move to the middle of nowhere unless there's something they want to get away from.'

She sighed through her nose, biting the inside of her cheek. Despite his questions, his attention on her made her heart dance like the aurora, but no way was she letting on how Javid was such a master manipulator that it had taken five years of her life for her to even realise how he was destroying her soul from within, and another two years to gather the strength to leave him. She felt stupid enough about all that as it was.

'I should go and dry my hair,' she told him, getting to her feet and stumbling instantly. He caught her wrists, drawing her close as he corrected her. 'Sorry...dizzy...' she managed, finding his piercing blue eyes in the steam. She swallowed again. 'I'll see you back outside the changing rooms?'

A woman she recognised from the table of people who'd been staring at them in the restaurant cornered her by the sinks. Mahlia pulled her robe tighter, trying to avoid her eyes, but the woman, who must be in her mid-forties stepped closer, ramming a hairbrush through her hair.

'You're brave,' she told her in the mirror. 'Going out on a date with Gunnar Johansson.'

'That's none of your business,' Mahlia told her curtly, towelling her own hair. It had already sprung back into its corkscrew curls.

The woman rolled her eyes. 'It's everyone's business what his family did to this country.'

'I don't really know the full details, but he seems like a good man to me,' she insisted, wondering if she should be saying anything at all.

The woman folded her arms. 'A good man?' She sniffed. 'I bet his ex-girlfriends don't think he's a good man. Don't they know what his family did? Watch out—that's all I'm saying.'

Mahlia frowned. 'Do you always attack people you don't know like this?'

The woman rolled her eyes, then sashayed off, leaving Mahlia shaken, gripping the sink.

'None of my business,' Mahlia reminded herself.

But her heart was wedged like a whole lemon in her throat and the woman's words about his ex-girlfriends—plural-stayed with her the whole drive home, as the craggy lava rocks slipped past and the lights came out to dance again ahead of them. It had been such a nice night...how dared someone try and spoil it?

Gunnar hadn't tried anything with her—he'd been nothing but a gentleman. But she *was* too trusting, too naive. Wasn't that what Javid had always said? He was probably right about that.

The feeling of lighter-than-air empowerment she'd felt in that lagoon, floating next to Gunnar, vanished like the northern lights as he pulled up at her door and said, 'I hope you have enough lip salve to last till we meet again.'

He was so good. So nice. Did he really go through women like hotcakes? *Ugh.*

Mahlia didn't want to be in the *slightest* bit affected by Gunnar Johansson. But already she knew she was probably in trouble.

CHAPTER FIVE

GUNNAR WAS EXHAUSTED. So was everyone. The rescue team had hiked the rough terrain for two hours already, scouring each turn and crevasse until their legs ached and their lungs burned.

The spectacular Njardarfal waterfall cascaded with fury up ahead. It tumbled in white blurry curtains down the rocky ledge, slamming into the foaming pool below. Its roar echoed off the crisp mountain air and was probably loosening more than a few snowdrifts.

Hopefully the man and his dog had taken shelter somewhere and weren't hurt, he thought, hunching against the wind. The missing man's partner had been beside himself in Reykjavik when they'd got the call. Leo, a thirty-six-year-old local man, had set out with his husky at six a.m., he'd said, and hadn't come back.

'Coffee?' Mahlia handed him the flask and he took it gratefully, feeling the hot liquid on the back of his parched throat.

She was still as striking as ever, with her cof-

fee-coloured skin against the white faux fur of
her hooded jacket, but she also looked tired. Her
eyes were black as obsidian, but with less of a
sparkle than he'd seen that night two weeks ago
when she'd looked all wonderstruck—and wet—
under the northern lights. He hadn't seen her
since—not to talk to, anyway. Only in passing.
He'd missed her, which surprised him.

It was always a kick, seeing people's eyes
light up when they saw the aurora, but there was
something interesting about this woman. Not just
her lilting New Zealand accent or those unbeliev-
ably sexy curves in a swimsuit. Her caution and
care, her burning ambition to help and change
lives, seemingly with every single venture she
attached herself to, was impressive.

The way she'd stared those people down in the
restaurant had touched him.

It took a lot to move him.

'We need two of you to go east,' Erik said now,
stopping just ahead at the crossroads on the lit-
tle-used hiking trail. 'Most people know not to
take this trail till summer, but we should check.'

'Maybe his dog shot off that way and he followed it,' Gunnar said. 'I've seen plenty of snow
foxes round these parts.'

'I'll go with Gunnar,' Mahlia said, glancing
his way, and he heard himself agreeing.

So she'd volunteered, before he'd suggested it,

he realised in surprise. He wasn't used to women wanting to go anywhere with him, what with his family legacy… But she was only a colleague, he reminded himself.

'We'll meet you back here in thirty?'

Mahlia shrugged her backpack straighter and followed him towards the falls, while Erik and Ásta turned north. With a pressing sense of urgency they began their search again, probing the crevices between large boulders as they approached the falls and scanning with their eyes for any sign of life. It wasn't snowing yet, but it was on the way. The sky hung low and grey.

'So, you've had a busy couple of weeks, huh?' she asked him now as they stepped over more rocks, testing the snow as they went.

He nodded. Yesterday he'd spent six hours straight alone with his mother, picking out paint for her kitchen while she swigged from a hip flask, thinking he didn't know she was doing it. Then he'd helped clean her house, because the cleaners had stopped coming months ago and she was always too drunk to do it herself.

He was supposed to be with his brother today, but here he was, and luckily Demus understood. His brother would have been right here with him if it weren't for the fact that his legs were giving out even more every year.

'How's your e-bike project going?' he asked

her now, remembering how she'd said she was doing it to help people like Demus.

'Pretty good,' she said, as they neared the falls. 'I had my meeting with the programme analyst. She says the data on most of the trails here is outdated. We're actually going to fly some of the prototypes over and use the new e-assist bikes to help gather new data, as soon as the snow clears. We're gathering volunteer bike riders at the moment, so we'll be trialling the bikes here *and* helping a nationwide data collection project at the same time.'

'That's really…wow…' he said, impressed yet again by her tenacity.

The snow wouldn't clear until June or July, but she was thinking of sticking around till then? Why did that suddenly make him feel equal parts excited and on edge? She definitely had a way of sticking in his brain. He still couldn't shake the idea that she was running away from something in New Zealand—that call she'd ignored in the car that first night had got him thinking. But maybe he was wrong. She liked to be alone, and there was nothing wrong with that. So did he, after everything his father had brought down on his head. Because of that, he was good at being paranoid, too. Too paranoid to mention Idina to Mahlia, at least…

His ex-girlfriend—the only woman he'd ever really loved—had not come up in a single one of their conversations about his past in California. It was better if she didn't, he supposed. He still couldn't keep all his emotions in check when he started down that path. Mahlia might look her up on the Internet and read about how she'd all but disappeared on him, thanks to the shame he'd brought upon her and the career she'd always wanted in politics.

Idina had kick-boxed her way into his heart on the way out of their class, back when things had been normal, about a year before the financial crash. Well, when things had been *his* version of normal. He hadn't known it at the time, but back in Iceland his father had been flying pop stars out to private yachts in Capri in an effort to acquire assets worth ten times the size of Iceland's economy.

Things had just been getting good with her when the news had broken about his father's arrest. The press had come down on Gunnar hard, reporting how he was out in California 'running from responsibility'. Even though he'd been there two years already. Some of the girls he'd met before Idina had told their 'story' for a quick buck. Idina, with her law degree pending and the political dream she'd had for ever under threat, hadn't been able to run from his life fast enough.

They still talked about him here, too. The women he dated never lasted long. As soon as they asked to meet his family he made his exit. He wouldn't do it to them! Anyone serious about him would only get dragged through the dirt along with him, like Idina had. Or they'd want to start a family with him. No, thanks. Kids…? With a name like his trailing behind them? What kind of life would they have? The more women's hearts he 'broke', the more people believed he was a serial player, so eventually he'd just stopped dating altogether.

Ma was still so broken by it all that she was trying to find the answers in the bottom of a bottle. She needed him…even if she never admitted it. And Demus… He was pretty self-sufficient, living on his own with the help of two carers who came in on alternate days, but there was barely a day that went by when he wasn't helping his older brother out with *something*.

A faint cry from up ahead made him stop in his tracks.

Mahlia grabbed his arm. 'Did you hear that?'

The cries grew louder as they hurried over rocks and boulders towards the roaring falls. The rush of the water almost made it too loud to hear much else.

'Stand back,' he told her, much to her visible annoyance.

He apologised quickly—was he being too protective? He knew he was overly protective of his mother and his brother—people he *cared* about, he realised. How quickly his protective instincts had grown to include Mahlia, even if she didn't seem to like it, he thought wryly, stepping over the crunchy dry snow towards the edge and straining his ears.

'Leo!' he yelled into the roar. 'Are you here?'

'Leo!' Mahlia was further along the ledge already, just behind him.

They yelled his name again. A dog's bark followed, only just audible above the water.

Then an answer. The man yelled out from below, the desperate plea of someone in pain.

'They're down there.'

Mahlia pointed into the falls as he reached her. He followed her stare down the snowy rock surface until his eyes fell on a figure, barely visible aside from a bright blue hat.

'I'll go. I know the way.'

'I'll go with you. He's hurt.'

'No. Wait here. I *know* this path,' he told her, but he could see the resolve in her eyes.

It reminded him of someone. Idina. Back when they'd met in that kick-boxing class. The ice cracked beneath his feet and the dog's barking upped in volume as he stepped down from one boulder to the next on what was a pathway to the bottom of the falls in the summer. Now, though, it was treacherous—even to people who knew the route down, like he did.

Water rushed over rocks as the waterfall grew louder to his right, his footsteps slid and earth and pine needles crunched underfoot as the dog's barking grew ever closer. He went for the rope, in case he had to lower himself down off the path to parts where there really was nowhere to stand. His foot slipped again.

'Damn....'

'Gunnar!' Mahlia's hand went for his arm. With a strength that defied her size she yanked him back and pushed him against the damp stone wall, flattening herself against it next to him, heaving for breaths.

What the...?

'You followed me,' he panted.

'Lucky I did,' she bit back.

But he saw the relief in her eyes, as well as a fierce determination to be seen and heard and acknowledged. It was like looking in a mirror.

'Look, he's just down there.'

They held each other's arms tight as they peered over the ledge together, the spray coating their faces like a thousand snakes spitting in fury. Leo was huddled there—what they could see of him, at least—beneath layers of weatherproof gear, just far enough away from the path to be unable to climb back up.

'I'll go down from here,' he told her, eyeing the terrain for something to tie a line to.

'Use this,' she said, motioning to a thick, ancient tree root protruding from the rocks just below.

He tested it out; it seemed strong enough.

'I'll help pull you back up.'

Mahlia was already on the radio, signalling their location to the others. Within moments Gunnar had lowered himself on the line and reached the grateful Leo, who was huddled beneath a rock shelf, shivering in pain. His foot was badly twisted, obviously broken or dislocated from his fall down into this isolated, windy corner.

'Mahlia, we need you,' he called up to her.

She was already hooked to the line, though, as if she'd done it a thousand times, proving once and for all that she didn't need the protection she seemed to inspire him to provide. It wasn't far—maybe two or three feet—and she was at his side in less than a minute, shrugging out of her backpack, checking Leo's leg.

'My dog…' He was wincing now. 'Katla. I was trying to reach her.'

Gunnar scanned the surroundings. All he could see was water. It was spraying his face and eyes, an ice bath he hadn't asked for. Then, down on the next ledge, he saw a beautiful young white husky, whimpering now instead of barking, probably sensing that her owner was finally getting help.

'I see her!'

'Can you reach her?'

Mahlia had wasted no time getting to work. With great skill and care, and lips visibly bluing from the cold, she was securing Leo's leg, soothing their shaken patient, making sure his pulse was strong, giving him water. All he seemed to care about, though, was his dog.

'I can reach her,' Gunnar said, helping Mahlia tie a tourniquet to Leo's leg so they could hoist him up more comfortably, and then securing another rope to a boulder.

It slipped several times before he caught it, and Mahlia rushed to help again, casting him an apprehensive frown. He told her with just one look that he was going for the dog, and that he'd be fine. He was met with a nod of silent acquiescence before she turned her attention back to sheltering Leo from the wind.

Her pretty face, slick and wet from the spray of the falls, was the last thing Gunnar saw as he lowered himself over the edge. Despite the situation, all he could do when he was out of sight was shake his head and smile. This woman was really something else…

* * *

From the looks on their faces, Gunnar could tell Erik and Ásta could hardly believe it when he and Mahlia emerged from the rocky lava field back onto the road, with a limping Leo and a bouncing white husky called Katla. She wasn't the first pet to be named after the island's most mysterious volcano.

'She's a little shaken, but she's not hurt,' Gunnar heard Mahlia telling them about the dog.

Ásta knelt to pet the thick-furred husky, being the animal fan she was, while he and Erik prepped a stretcher for Joe. The rescue truck was already waiting, its doors open wide. The snow had started up again now, and Gunnar watched Mahlia intently as he packed up his lines quickly, listening as she spoke, mesmerised by how capable and engaged she was with everything around her.

He could only thank the heavens he'd been lucky enough to have someone like her join him out there. She was fearless.

Not that he was going to do a damn thing about this unfortunate attraction. What had started out as a dinner with a colleague had turned into something more on his part—a need to know more about her. But with that would come more questions from her; she would want an intro into more of his world, which never did anyone any good. She had too much going for her to be burdened by his reputation.

At the hospital, he and Mahlia waited anxiously for the results of Leo's scan.

'Have you been a dog-sitter before?' he asked her, gesturing to Katla at her feet.

They hadn't been allowed any further than the waiting room with the young husky, but there was no one else to watch her; Ásta and Erik were already en-route back to their homes, to shower off the cold that had kept them all out there for most of the morning.

He was trying not to watch the clock. He really had to get back to Demus if there was still any hope of them making it to the cabin in the few hours of daylight they had left. He'd promised him barbecued lamb chops and a soak in the hot tub. It always helped Demus relax, took *some* of his pain away. But it didn't seem fair to leave Mahlia alone here…waiting.

Mahlia ran a hand over the dog's rug-like back, and he watched her slender fingers sinking into the white fur.

'My husband would never allow me…us…to get a dog,' she said sadly.

Then she bit down hard on her lip and adjusted herself on the hard plastic seat. Gunnar turned to her. Her face was strained as she stared at the floor, her eyes pinched, her lips pressed together into a frown. There was no wedding ring on her finger.

'Your husband?'

'Technically he's still my husband, but we're separated,' she said tightly, dragging a hand through her curls.

Gunnar felt the muscles in his brow pulling together as he struggled not to ask what had happened. It was none of his business. Instead, he said, 'He wouldn't *allow* you to get a dog? You make it sound like you wanted one and the man just stood in your way.'

'It wasn't practical...not with my lifestyle,' she followed up, too quickly. 'I didn't have the time. I didn't know how to care for a dog properly. I couldn't have given a dog what it needed.'

'OK...'

He nodded, soaking it all in. There was something in her demeanour now, not just in her words, that told him she was repeating what someone else had told her—an opinion that wasn't entirely hers. Maybe she wasn't so fearless about *everything*.

'But aren't you always outdoors on your bikes?' he pressed. 'Dogs love joining in with exercise.'

Mahlia shrugged. 'I couldn't have taken it to the hospital with me, though, could I? When I worked a twelve-hour shift? And Javid wouldn't have taken it out. He hates dogs.'

'Javid...' he repeated softly, pondering the sudden apathy in her voice and studying the soft sheen of her heart-shaped mouth. That was the name he'd seen on her phone that night in the car.

He should shut the hell up and butt out of her business, but intrigue made his tongue loosen. 'How long were you married to Javid?'

She paused a few breaths. 'Seven years. We still *are* married, like I said. Stubborn ass won't sign the divorce papers.'

'I get it. OK...' He stared at his hands in his lap. So, her ex had—still did have—some kind of twisted hold on her. *That* was what she was running away from.

The door was flung open. A broad man in a ski jacket burst through, bringing a flurry of snow in with him. Right away, Katla leapt from the floor. She pounced on him, jumping, barking, dancing, her bushy tail wagging a million miles an hour.

'Leo's partner,' they said in unison, rising to greet him.

The burly man, who introduced himself as Gisli, lowered his hood, fussing over the husky in relief as he asked the woman at the front desk where Leo was.

'We're waiting to hear if it's a break or a dislocation, but it seems he got off pretty lightly,' Gunnar explained.

'You were the ones who rescued him?

Gunnar nodded curtly as the guy seemed to recognise him. He saw Mahlia's eyes bounce between them. Would Gisli take a step backwards? he wondered. Turn his head to see who'd noticed them interacting? He never knew what to expect, bearing a name like his. Thankfully, this man was different.

Gisli thrust his hand out at him, then drew him into a grateful, manly embrace with the strength of a bear. 'Thank you, thank you, thank you,' he gushed. 'He probably would have died if it wasn't for you, Dr Johansson.'

Gunnar cleared his throat, stepped backwards, brushing the snow off his front as Mahlia bit back a smile.

'Mahlia was with me. She helped patched him up and helped carry him from the waterfall. And the rest of our team…'

'Well, then, I offer you my eternal gratitude too, Mahlia. That man…he's the love of my life…'

Gisli extended to Mahlia the same form of heartfelt appreciation, pulling her into a tight embrace that made her smile. She hugged him back as he sniffed emotionally against her shoulder.

'You have no idea…'

A nurse came to inform them that it was a dislocation and not a break, as they had feared. Leo would now receive treatment to ease the pain and they could visit him soon. They were assured that he'd be back on his feet before long. Although maybe he shouldn't be hiking for a while—and definitely never alone.

'He knows not to go out alone,' Gisli grumbled, ruffling Katla's ears. 'He thought Katla would protect him, but she's young, you know?'

'The husky *did* need a bit of help too,' Mahlia explained. 'Gunnar went down a few more feet to another ledge to get her. He was quite incredible, considering the force of the water and…'

She trailed off quickly and flushed. Gunnar kept a straight face, even as his heart performed a strange shift that sent his blood to places he'd rather it didn't go in public. Whether she was saying it because she'd seen the way some people treated him, or because she really thought he was 'incredible' shouldn't matter, but it did. His pulse was leaping and falling like a pair of fish on a line.

Gisli gasped dramatically, as if he'd just remembered something. 'We will have you both over for dinner. Soon. When Leo's had some rest. Do you like reindeer?'

He fixed his eyes on Mahlia, who stuttered, 'I… Reindeer? I don't know.'

'We just had one butchered and frozen. I make a very good stew. I insist.'

Gunnar was trying his best not to laugh at the look on her face as Gisli asked for his number, so that he could send them both an invitation, and was led away by the nurse. The nurse told them her assistant would look after the dog till her owner returned, or one of them, and that Katla would be fine.

Gunnar was just telling himself that Gisli would probably never call when Mahlia turned to him from her phone. The look on her face told him she'd had some disappointing news.

'Everything OK?'

She sighed. 'One of the guys who signed up for the e-bike trial has had to pull out. He's had a relapse, and his physician doesn't think it's smart for him to make any commitments. I was planning to go and meet with him now, but...' She looked at him askance. 'I guess I'll have to spend my birthday afternoon doing something else.'

Birthday?

Gunnar released the breath that had somehow got lodged in his windpipe. He'd been about to excuse himself and make for his car, but now... 'It's your birthday?'

She bobbed her head, shrugged.

'Today?' he followed up, incredulous.

She'd accepted this search call-out on her

birthday. She could've been in a spa, or on a Golden Circle trip, or any of the other things tourists did in Iceland to have themselves a fairy-tale day.

'Yes, today.'

His mind was racing now. 'Happy birthday. Do you have a back-up plan?'

She laughed. 'In a place where I know next to no one? Sure—let me just gather all my besties.'

He felt his mouth twitch with a hint of a smile. Sarcasm suited her. 'In that case, how would you like to join me for dinner? We can celebrate your birthday and make up for the lost e-bike trial participant at the same time. Sound good?'

Mahlia's mouth flew open for a second, and then she closed it. The surprise on her face made his heart swell with warmth and anticipation, even though involving anyone in his messed-up family life was actually the last thing he should be doing.

A smile lit up her face suddenly. It made him forget everything and wonder what it might be like to kiss her.

'OK,' she said softly. 'That sounds like a nice idea…thank you.'

Excitement bubbled in Gunnar's chest, erupting into a goofy grin that he quickly suppressed behind his hand. He'd worry about his dumb decisions later—it was her birthday!

'There's one catch. We have to drive fifteen minutes out of town. And we have to bring my brother.'

'Your brother?' Mahlia grabbed her bag and slung it over one shoulder.

'I promised Demus we'd hang out at the cabin—fire up the grill, maybe take a dunk in the hot tub,' he said, walking her to the door. He opened it for her.

'Hot tub?' she repeated, and he didn't miss her glance at him, or the way she bit her lip thoughtfully.

Hopefully she wasn't thinking he just wanted to get her in a bathing suit again. Then again, she wasn't exactly hard on the eyes, fully dressed or not.

Touching her arm lightly, he noticed for the first time how small she was compared to him; it made him feel even more protective of her.

'What are you grilling?' she asked.

'I promise no reindeer,' he said, yanking on his hat. 'Not that I don't recommend it. It's very high in protein.'

'I wouldn't say no to trying it…'

Of course you wouldn't.

Mahlia stepped with him out into the snow. She pulled up her hood and her curls flew from it, whipping his cheek for just a second. The feeling sent an unexplainable warmth right through him. Then, as he slid into the car beside her, another pang of apprehension struck him.

They made small talk as he drove. From what he knew so far, she was warm and kind and fascinating. He also saw in her bravery and vulnerability—two qualities he admired in a woman. There was a certain captivating mystery to her wholesome aura, too, and he found himself wanting to learn even more. Who wouldn't want to know more?

Trusting her enough to take her with him to meet Demus, though, had surprised him the second he'd suggested it. What the hell was he doing, inviting a woman he barely knew to the cabin to meet his brother? A married woman, no less, with a controlling husband at large? He could only imagine what had driven Mahlia all the way here to Iceland.

Ah, chill out, he told himself. It wasn't as if she wanted to sell a story about his messed-up mother or force him to continue his doomed legacy by popping out his babies…not like the last girl he'd gone out on only three dates with.

This wasn't even a date. And anyway, she was barely out of a marriage.

Mahlia probably wanted nothing from him. And the second she knew more about him, she never would.

CHAPTER SIX

THE DRIVE IN the fluttering snow was breathtakingly beautiful, even as Mahlia's heart thumped with trepidation. What was she doing, accepting this invitation? All she knew was that some long-forgotten part of her had spoken up about it being her birthday almost in the hope that Gunnar would ask her out, and now the recklessness of her actions was already threatening to bite her in the backside. She barely knew him. And if Javid ever found out...

Gah! He has no hold on you now, she reminded herself, focusing in on Demus in the rear-view mirror.

He looked like Gunnar but a few years older. His hair was darker, his chin sharper and his body slimmer, but the resemblance was there. He was chatting to his brother from the back of the wheelchair-adaptable SUV.

Mahlia couldn't understand a word either of them was saying, but the rhythm and cadence of the Icelandic language sounded like music to her ears. It was lilting and lyrical. The gentle, rolling quality of the words in Gunnar's deep baritone reminded her of waves crashing on a shore.

Oh, no. Just as she was relaxing… There was her phone again.

'You OK?' Gunnar glanced at her, frowning, as she clutched at her bag.

She was trying to ignore the perpetual vibration on her lap. There was no way she was answering. Javid could take a running jump. If she turned it off, though, he would know she was ignoring him; he'd be so angry. He'd never sign the divorce papers if she enraged him. Her stomach knotted the way it had been trained to do at the mere *thought* of any adverse reaction from him.

'I'm great,' she answered chirpily, meeting Demus's liquid blue eyes in the mirror. 'Thank you for inviting me on your boys' night.'

Demus laughed. 'We're happy to have you. You know Gunnar just wants to show you how long he can stand shirtless in the snow while he flips the lamb chops on the grill.'

'I'm not going to get dressed every time I climb out of the hot tub,' Gunnar reasoned.

She felt herself flush as he glanced at her, picturing him with his shirt off again.

'And anyway,' he continued, '*you* can't wait to show Mahlia how terrible you are on the piano.'

'I blame my useless hands,' Demus replied, holding up his fingers.

'They've always been useless,' Gunnar teased, but the love and respect in his eyes for his brother spoke volumes about how he really felt.

She'd already seen how Demus's hands had trembled slightly when he'd tried to open a pack of gum earlier. The look of intense concentration on his face had eventually given way to irritation and pain. Gunnar had reached over and taken the packet from him, deftly opening it before handing it back.

She smiled at the way they teased each other, too—at their easy familiarity and tenderness towards one another, despite their differences. They laughed often in between words. There was a good-natured camaraderie that underscored their shared bloodline. In a way, it kind of made her envious. She'd often wondered if a sibling in her life would have changed anything...been someone to talk to who might have steered her away from Javid, noticed she was changing, suffocating, when so many of her friends hadn't.

She'd hidden it too well.

The snow-capped mountains that ringed the cabin looked like something off a postcard. The hot tub sat on a deck that looped around the small two-bedroom structure, and Gunnar had it steaming and bubbling in no time. The whole of the tiny place had been adapted for Demus's wheel-chair; there were ramps to every room. It wasn't as flashy as she'd imagined, judging by the apart-ment building he lived in in Reykjavik. It was cosy, and homely, and felt full of love. As if they'd had a lot of happy times here before…

But the last thing she needed right now was to get emotionally invested in a man—look where that had got her till now.

Hiding out in Iceland, that's where!

Still, Gunnar looked like the picture of Viking masculinity as he stood at the grill, piling on lamb chops and seasoning chicken fillets, while she and Demus helped prepare a salad in the kitchen. She watched him through the kitchen widow, bent over the flame in the orange glow of a heated lamp.

The ubiquitous knitted cream and brown Ice-landic sweater he'd picked up from the back of the couch and thrown on was like nothing she'd seen him in so far. It looked almost a little old and bedraggled. Loved, like the cabin. She wanted to feel the wool on her face, snuggle into it. He probably gave the best cuddles…

Demus caught her looking at Gunnar. 'What's going on, then?' he asked her, rinsing tomatoes and lettuce in a bowl on the specially low-placed workbench. 'Are you dating my brother?'

There was a certain wariness to his voice that suddenly set her on edge.

'No,' she said, too quickly.

'He hasn't invited anyone here before,' Demus said thoughtfully, his hands shaking around the lettuce leaves. 'Not even Idina. Not that she'd have left California anyway, even before it all went wrong. Too much of a valley girl. You know, I only met the woman once before…this.' He gestured to his fragile body in the wheelchair. 'If I'd known then how badly she was going to treat him… Don't believe everything you read about Gunnar, Mahlia. Or what people around here might tell you.'

He put the bowl of salad down on the workbench a little too hard. Through the window, Gunnar looked up at the sound, his face instantly swallowed by smoke.

Mahlia's heart was in her throat, but she feigned ambivalence. Obviously she'd been thinking about it, wondering if that lady's comments at the Blue Lagoon had been true…about how Gunnar tore through women. This was the first time she'd heard the name Idina. So that was what he'd left behind in California…

'He hasn't told me anything about her… Idina,' she said carefully. 'And why should he? We barely know each other, really.'

'Indeed,' Demus said, but a smile hovered on his lips.

'I form my own opinions anyway,' she followed up. 'I know he's a good man. And I know what it's like to be scrutinised and judged for something you haven't even had the *chance* to do yet.'

She shut her mouth. Demus stared at her a moment longer, as if sizing her up. Even as he nodded, her heart was like a wild bird, just from thinking how Javid had stolen her confidence, made her believe she was incompetent, small, incapable, worthless, *less than*. If either of these men knew how she'd lost herself in his shadow, they'd think she was an idiot. But then, maybe Gunnar had been through something similar, but on a global scale, after his family name had been trodden into the dirt. Maybe Demus had too—as if he wasn't dealing with enough now.

You never knew what a person was hiding behind their tough facade. Idina had clearly been someone special. Someone who'd hurt Gunnar...

'Food's ready!' Gunnar called.

Demus saluted him and Mahlia watched as Demus moved his hands in front of her, flexing and unflexing them before trying and failing to open the bottle he'd just pulled from a cupboard. The juxtaposition between the strength of his arms and the frailty of his fingers was stark—an all too familiar sight to Mahlia. She had seen it before in people with multiple sclerosis.

She took the bottle gently, loosened the cap and handed it back. He unscrewed it and sniffed it, pulling a face that made her laugh. 'Moonshine never gets any better,' he said.

'Then why drink it?'

He rolled his eyes and grinned. 'We're Vikings, baby.'

She laughed, carrying the salad past the piano and a well-worn couch to the table as he balanced the bottle and three mugs on his lap in the wheelchair.

Maybe she should ask Demus if he wanted to take part in the e-assist trial, she thought. Gunnar had said they both enjoyed cycling. She'd wanted to ask Gunnar the second the other guy had pulled out, but something had stopped her. Perhaps a fear of getting closer to him…involving herself in his world?

That wasn't why she was here, she reminded herself firmly, taking a seat at the sturdy wooden table by the roaring fire. Even if she had pretty much forced him to invite her somewhere today.

Maybe she shouldn't have done it.

God, stop beating yourself up, woman, just because Javid's not here to do it for you. It is your birthday. It's not like this is going to be a regular thing.

Demus lit three red candles in the centre of the table as Gunnar walked in with a giant plate of meat, the epitome of swoon-worthy masculinity. Gosh, he was ridiculously good-looking, she thought, swallowing as he caught her eye in the candlelight. How could a man be this gorgeous? This would definitely have to be a one-time thing. She wasn't going to be another of his brief flings. Though she somehow doubted he was as callous as that woman in the changing room had made him out to be, what if he came to have so much of a hold on her that she literally *couldn't* leave him?

OK, so she was getting way ahead of herself, but nope. Never again. Never, ever, ever would she put herself in that position—not for anything. So what if having a family one day was something she still dared to dream about? Maybe she'd get a donor, or adopt—whatever it took to have a child on her own. A man wasn't necessary for that any more. Anyway, right now being single was definitely what she needed...even if the way Gunnar's blue eyes holding hers put her on edge in the most exciting way.

An hour later, with her belly warm and full, she sat back in the hot tub, thrilling at Gunnar's gaze flickering to her cleavage as he offered her a drink.

'What is it this time?' she asked.

'A different kind of moonshine,' Demus answered for him, stretching his arms out in the water.

Gunnar had carried him here carefully, lowering him gently down to a special raised seat, and she'd bitten the inside of her cheek, watching every corded muscle in his broad shoulders straining, dripping with hot water.

'How many kinds are there?'

'The bad kind, and the absolutely intolerable kind,' Gunnar said, toasting her and then Demus with his cup, then discarding it without taking so much as a sip. He was going to have to drive them home after all.

Already she didn't want to leave. The sky was clear now. The stars shifted above them against a velvety sky like brilliant diamonds. Everything seemed more vivid out here. She took a sip of her drink from the thick ceramic mug, eyeing the surrounding mountains, willing the northern lights to come out and dance. This moonshine was so powerful, it almost tasted as if it had been distilled twice—firstly on earth and then again in the pits of hell. The taste was intense, and both brothers laughed at the look on her face.

'It's awful,' she conceded. But she took another sip as her phone vibrated from inside the cabin, wishing she had the courage to just turn it off completely.

'Want me to get that for you?' Gunnar offered.

'No, it's fine, really,' she said hurriedly, ignoring the look of confusion he threw her way—or was that suspicion?

While she wanted to see as much of his bare, muscled torso as possible, she did not need to see Javid's name on her screen.

Instead, she let the moonshine warm her from the inside, feeling it spreading outwards through every crevice of her body like liquid fire. It burned all the way down to her stomach, leaving behind a lingering warmth. She felt alive and invigorated, especially in the spotlight of Gunnar's gaze…but also as if something more dangerous was brewing.

He knew she was running away by coming to Iceland. She'd told him too much earlier, at the hospital, about how Javid had never 'allowed' her to get a dog. The indignation in his eyes—all over his face, in fact—had shaken her. It had been as if he was personally offended that someone could be so controlling…that she'd let anyone dictate what was best for her.

Gunnar was a protector, not a dictator, that much she could tell. But who was Idina to him? What had happened with her in California?

* * *

It felt as if they'd sat there for hours. Gunnar would occasionally point out constellations or stars that were especially bright, explaining their stories laced with Icelandic myths and legends.

When he labelled one star her 'birthday star', flashing her that jokey grin that was starting to show itself more and more tonight, her heart leapt and bucked. This was something special she was experiencing now; she was feeling things she hadn't expected to ever feel. For a second she found herself wondering what Gunnar might be like as a father, teaching two little kids to start the hot tub, flip chicken on the grill.

What?

She caught herself. Two kids. That had always been her dream. A boy and girl. But, as she'd already decided, she did *not* need a man for that!

Demus announced that he'd drunk too much and was going for a nap.

'So much for your piano concert,' Gunnar teased, before carrying him inside to the couch by the fire.

Mahlia tried not to look as if she was staring at the hot liquid steaming off his shoulder blades as he strode across the deck. But when he walked back outside several minutes later she found herself eyeing him through the steam, holding her breath. They were alone. And, to her horror, he was holding her phone.

'Seventy-eight missed calls from Javid?' Gunnar handed the phone to her, almost laughing. 'The guy must really want to talk to you. Maybe he signed your divorce papers?'

'Yeah, right...'

Mahlia clambered out of the hot tub, limbs dripping water onto the deck. Mortified and embarrassed, she snatched the phone from his hand, but her wet fingers slipped before she could grip it. It tumbled past them into the hot, bubbling water.

For a moment she froze, staring as it sank to the bottom. She considered the fact that she was more relieved in this moment than annoyed, actually. Funny, that. But Gunnar was already diving for it. She watched in shock as he emerged with the gadget like King Triton from a well, shaking off a treasure.

'Lucky it's waterproof,' he said, turning it around in his big hands.

She stepped back into the hot tub, meeting him in the middle of the pool. Their fingers brushed as she took the phone from him and glanced at the screen. If only it wasn't waterproof, she thought in dismay. He was right. Seventy-eight missed calls.

Just a few moments on the deck had been

enough to ice her blood, and now she couldn't seem to move. It felt just as if Javid was here, yelling at her from behind the phone's screen to call him back. And yet Gunnar's handsome wet face was inches from hers.

Two different worlds.

'I'm not calling him back,' she told the blue of his eyes, before she could think.

'Do you really just never talk to him?' he asked as she finally forced her hand to put the phone down on the side of the tub.

'Not if I can help it.'

'Why don't you just block his number?'

She swallowed, turning back to him, feeling even smaller now. It was a good enough question. If only she *could* block his number. Ignoring him was a little passive, she knew that, but if she blocked him altogether he would come for her. It would be worse. He'd just be more angry...or he'd do the whole emotional manipulation thing: crying, begging her not to leave him, not to have her attorney take it further.

The whole situation was a mess. To get a default judgement from the court she'd probably have to prove the breakdown of the marriage and his mental cruelty. The thought of recounting it all, hearing herself admit what a weak pushover she'd been all this time, was debilitating.

Gunnar was still waiting for an answer. The

warmth of his gaze pressed against her skin like a physical touch before the moonshine loosened her tongue.

'A conversation with Javid always goes one way,' she told him on a sigh. 'Besides, I don't want to be constantly reminded of our failed marriage when I'm trying *so* hard to move on from it.'

Gunnar growled in agreement, the sound drawn from deep within his chest. He towered over her as he reached for her fingers, holding them in his own large, warm hand, sending electricity coursing through her body, lighting up every molecule of her being.

'I know what it's like…trying to move on from something, and feeling like you just…can't.'

His words came out as if he'd wrestled them from the depths of his heart. He was staring into her eyes now, as if she was the only thing that mattered in this moment. The sudden rush of something more powerful than she was ready for consumed her.

'Is that what you had to do with Idina?'

A look of sadness flashed across his features and she kicked herself for mentioning her, but that look just now, and the way he'd gripped her fingers…that was way too intense.

'How do you know about her? Go on—tell me

what you've read,' he said, sinking back against the edge of the tub.

'Nothing,' she said, while her world rearranged itself. 'Demus told me there was someone called Idina, in California.'

His jaw shifted as he lowered himself further into the steamy water. 'He did, huh? Well, I guess it's not surprising the love of my life ran for the hills as soon she learned what had happened with my father. Who'd want to be involved with all that?'

Mahlia sank against the side of the tub wall, suddenly too hot. 'She left you?'

'I told you before that I stayed in California after it happened. But she was gone the second the press descended—before Dad was even sentenced. She wanted a career in politics, and she couldn't risk all that being snatched away because of my family's reputation.'

So that's what happened, she thought.

Idina had freaked out, left him, and broken his heart. He'd stayed there and dealt with everything alone. God, poor Gunnar.

Behind him, the faintest trace of green was lighting up the sky above the mountains. 'I've only met you and Demus, but so far I *like* your family,' she told him.

He snorted, sending bubbles her way. 'Demus is the only sane one left besides me.'

'You said your mother worked in television?'

'No, I didn't say that.'

She grimaced. Maybe she'd read that on the Internet.

Busted.

Gunnar frowned. 'She never worked again after the network fired her. And Dad... Well, I don't know how much you've read about him, but he's somewhere in Asia now. I don't know where. Last I heard it was Cambodia.'

'What's he doing there?'

'Your guess is as good as mine.'

Mahlia bit down on her cheek, wishing she'd never asked.

What a mess.

'Well, for what it's worth, Gunnar, this is the best birthday I've ever had,' she told him anyway, watching the neon green light behind him start to spread and separate into ethereal strands and swirl amongst the stars. 'Should we run from the monsters yet?'

He followed her eyes to the sky, then moved beside her again, shoulder to shoulder. The tension fizzed between them as the lights started dancing like a private show just for them.

He nudged her gently. 'I think the monsters will let you off, seeing as it's your birthday. Sorry for unloading all that on you.'

'Don't be sorry,' she said, trying to ignore the shiver of anticipation at his touch.

'Is it really the best birthday you've ever had?'

She smiled softly, buoyed by the heat of him and the water, and the lingering buzz of the drinks. 'Two birthdays ago I was locked in a bathroom at a theatre, crying. I'd say this is much better.'

'Why were you crying in a bathroom?' He was visibly appalled.

'Javid always made the plans for my birthday,' she told the sky, aware of Gunnar's every breath beside her.

His closeness both settled her and sent hundreds of fluttering Monarch butterflies on a frenzied path through her stomach.

'I was never allowed to see my friends. He always took me to some opera he wanted us to be seen at. I didn't know how to admit to my friends that he was so controlling; they never knew. I let them think I *wanted* to be at the opera instead of the dinner they'd booked for me.'

Gunnar was silent. The northern lights kept swirling.

'Some of them stopped talking to me after a while,' she told him, wondering why she was still speaking.

'I've lost a few friends myself over the years,' he said. 'But… Mahlia, I'm so sorry you got caught up in a relationship like that. I don't blame you for getting out of it.'

'If only I could!' She half laughed. 'I had to tell my solicitor where I am, so of course Javid knows I'm in Iceland, too. I wake up every day thinking today's the day he'll track me down and demand I come home.'

To her shock, Gunnar reached for her face, turning her attention from the sky. Her breath caught as his fingers lingered on her jaw, his gaze intense and full of a fire that kick-started a riot in her belly.

'You don't have to worry about him coming here,' he growled. 'He's not going to get anywhere close to you. I can promise you that. Not while I'm around.'

Mahlia stared into his eyes, too stunned to speak. A spark of hope sprang up within her, rising like an ocean around her pounding heart. For the first time in years she truly believed that she could and would escape Javid's oppressive grip.

Was Gunnar actually going to kiss her?

His hand moved up to gently caress her cheek, sending shivers down her spine. She wanted nothing more than for him to close the gap between them and seal their lips together with the northern lights flickering above them. But just as he leaned closer nerves got the better of her. What was she getting herself into here? Everything she'd vowed she hadn't come here looking for? She was being so naive. This was how it had all started with Javid! The trust, his warmth, his desire to 'protect' her…

Make that control her.

So why did this feel so good?

Conflicted she pressed her hands to his warm chest, biting back a laugh. 'To think I so wanted to have his babies. I couldn't wait to start a family. He knew it too—knew how much I wanted to be a mother. But he kept putting it off. He'd say, "Not yet. It's not the right time for us, Mahlia." I'm lucky he did. I mean…imagine him being a father. The man's incapable of caring for anyone other than himself.'

She shut her mouth, realising Gunnar had retreated. He'd backed off again, settled at the other side of the tub, and was watching her cautiously. Oh, no. Why on earth had she said all that? She wasn't that drunk…was she?

It was just so overwhelming: him, this magical moment, the newness of it all, finally hearing him speak more openly about his past and getting some of the load off her own chest.

He'd been going to kiss her. Or maybe he hadn't. Had she just misread him completely?

'I'm so sorry, Gunnar. I'm not used to talking about him, or any of this. I don't know what to say,' she admitted, letting out a nervous laugh. 'You must think I'm crazy.'

Gunnar was watching her with an unreadable expression on his face now. 'You don't have to say anything,' he said softly, as she cringed inside. 'But no. I don't think you're crazy. You're special to have come through something like that and survived—do you know that?'

Mahlia could have died! They were colleagues, and she was married—there were so many reasons why he might have backed off. But the way he'd said 'you're special', as though it were an indisputable fact instead of mere words, had only sent her heart into even more of a riot.

When they emerged from the hot tub a little later she was cold to the bone, even inside by the fire and with her clothes back on. Gunnar went to wake Demus, and she resisted helping him get his brother into the wheelchair. It was something he obviously enjoyed managing on his own.

'What were you two talking about out there?' Demus asked, yawning and pulling his hat over his head.

'Nothing,' Gunnar said, shooting her a look that made the shame of her revelations flare back into her brain.

The heat from the tub had made the moonshine go to her head. Now, on solid ground, she was stone-cold sober. What an idiot she was, spilling her heart and soul when she barely knew him. Her worries seemed so trivial compared to the pain he'd revealed. His girlfriend had put her career prospects above their relationship and left him to cope with a global scandal alone. His brother was in a wheelchair, and his mother… well, who knew how she was managing? And yet here Mahlia was, pretty much admitting she'd messed up her life through her own cowardice and poor judgement in men.

No wonder he'd backed off!

Helplessly she sat on the couch, watching Demus go round in the wheelchair, turning off the lights. The cold had got into her bones. When he saw her shivering, Gunnar handed her the knitted sweater he'd been wearing earlier, and she pulled it on gratefully over her own.

'This is nice,' she said, breathing in the scent of it.

It calmed her. It smelled like him…like this cabin…like woodsmoke, pine and a sweetness she couldn't define.

'It was my great-grandfather's,' Gunnar told her, crouching to put out the fire in the hearth. 'He spent his whole life in a small fishing village off the coast.'

'Up north,' Demus added. 'It's beautiful up

there, with the whales all swarming round the boats.'

They explained how their great-grandmother had knitted the sweater by hand, with wool from their Icelandic sheep, to keep her husband warm in Iceland's unforgiving winter months. The images they painted without even trying made her smile. And the fact that he trusted her to wear such a precious heirloom warmed her as much as the wool. He thought she was 'special.'

Then she remembered again how she'd ruined the moment outside and the shame crashed back in.

It didn't leave her for the whole drive back to Reykjavik. She would never, ever stop cringing inside over everything she'd blurted out. As if he needed to take on her problems after everything he'd been through himself!

Which reminded her... She should have asked this question before...

'Demus,' she ventured, turning to him. 'I have a place open on the e-assist trial, so if you'd like to, maybe you can join it?'

She hadn't asked Gunnar if Demus might be interested, fearing it might seem as if she was trying to get involved in his life, when she knew he kept his cards close to his chest about his family, but she'd been invited to come here with the brothers today, hadn't she?'

'I'd love to know more about it,' Demus said enthusiastically. 'Gunnar's told me about what you're doing. Did he tell you how I used to beat him in every bike race?'

'In your dreams!'

The two started up their brotherly banter again, and before she left the car Mahlia promised to be in touch about the trial. Gunnar's gaze lingered over her lips before she closed the passenger door. He was probably thinking how glad he was that he hadn't kissed a crazy person tonight. But he had talked about her venture with his brother before...

Interesting.

This news helped her shame abate a little, even if she was still reeling over how she'd just proved how right Javid had been when he'd told her... What was it? That a woman like her was 'wholly unattractive to most men'.

She shouldn't care what Gunnar thought of her—he wasn't why she'd come here. He was too complicated, and she was not available! Even so, she clean forgot to look at her phone again.

She didn't take the sweater off either.

CHAPTER SEVEN

THE CALL CAME in at four minutes past six a.m. Gunnar was already on his second cup of coffee. Erik gave him the update as he drove to the hangar, and he turned up the heat inside the truck to beat off the draught of icy air at the edges of his scarf. The snow flurry was unrelenting around his windscreen. It had been snowing non-stop for the last two days. Getting anywhere fast this morning would be impossible.

To think just three nights ago, out at the cabin, they'd had clear skies. Clear enough for him to see way more of Mahlia than he'd expected to. He'd seen inside her head—enough to realise exactly how emotionally abused she'd been by her ex. She wasn't something he could fix; he had enough on his plate. She wasn't staying here, and she definitely wasn't fling material. She wasn't like anyone else he'd ever met...

Shaking that near-kiss from his head—again— he focused on the road and on Erik's voice. The blizzard last night had rendered the small village of Hvítaeyri on the Víkurfjall mountainside unreachable, which wasn't unusual at this time of year. But in this case, a twenty-eight-year-old pregnant woman called Helga had just gone into labour. They needed to get her medical attention stat, which meant flying the chopper in as soon as possible.

'You're here—good man.'

Erik greeted him at the hangar, head bent against the howling wind and snow. He was talking on the radio now, Gunnar assumed with someone at the village. Mahlia's car pulled up with a slight screech. He found himself watching her as she exited with a slam of the door and hurried for shelter, huddling into her scarf.

'We've done rescues like this before, but she might be too far into labour by the time we get there for us to get her out,' Ásta was saying to him and their pilot, Sven. 'We really need a midwife, but the only volunteer we know is away…'

'I can deliver the baby if I have to,' Mahlia said.

Gunnar swung around.

'I've done it before.'

She brushed the snow from her hood and met his eyes. A flicker of caution crossed her face—at seeing him, probably—but then she straight-

ened up, folded her arms, all business, and asked
Erik for the latest.

He had to admit, whatever she'd gone through
with that idiot Javid she was a force of nature.
He'd delivered a baby before too—once. All phy-
sicians received basic obstetrics training in the
US, as part of their clinical rotations. It didn't
mean he'd enjoyed it. It had made him dwell
on all the things he'd never have, thanks to his
messed-up family.

What did Mahlia think, now she knew about
how Idina had left him? The press were still
relentless in their pursuit of him. There was a
story about every woman he was seen with, either printed, blasted all over the Internet, or shot
from someone's loud mouth. Hopefully the vultures wouldn't get to her, too. All the more reason to be very careful...

Ásta and Sven began to brief Mahlia on what
to expect when they reached the village. They
said she might have to be lowered on the winch,
with him.

Gunnar focused on her face. She didn't look
scared—far from it. If anything, she seemed res-
olute, determined to help this woman and her
baby no matter the cost. A new wave of respect
washed over him as she helped them stow the
medical gear onto the chopper.

An hour later, the snow had subsided enough

for them to take off. Mahlia sat opposite him and didn't meet his eyes.

'How are you doing?' he asked her, over the whir of the blades.

He'd spent the last hour prepping the winch and fielding calls, and she'd been talking with Ásta. He wondered if she'd been avoiding him since that night. Since he'd made it awkward for her...on his territory.

'I'm good,' she said tightly. 'Sorry I haven't been in touch about the trial yet. I'm still trying to line up potential times for Demus to meet Inka, the programme analyst I told you about. She's been away in Spain.'

He nodded, told her it was fine, although he wanted to say she could have been in touch to tell him that. She was definitely avoiding him. He watched her profile as she studied the mountains through the windows, her curls flapping around her hood. Was she still wearing his sweater under that coat?

It was shameful how much he'd wanted to kiss her in the hot tub the other night. He'd taken a vulnerable woman out to the middle of nowhere and made a move. Well, almost made a move. Maybe he would've done if she hadn't mentioned that she wanted a family. That had snapped him back to his senses.

Not only was taking a married colleague to

his private retreat the kind of behaviour to get everyone talking more nonsense about him, if they found out about it, but he would never have children. She was too special a person to be fling material, and too vulnerable to involve in all his family drama—she was trying to rebuild her own life! He'd made the right decision, backing off.

They were nearing the village already. Mahlia was applying the lip salve he'd given her that first night, talking with Erik, making plans, focused and determined to help this woman any way she could.

That was the kind of thing he wanted to be known for too—making a difference to people's lives, not wasting the time of someone who wanted more from him than he could give. There'd been that fashion designer, Frida, a couple of years ago. He'd liked her, and she hadn't been that bothered that he'd never let her meet his mother. Ma had been was causing a stir in the media at the time, showing up drunk for her yoga classes.

Then Frida had started hinting at marriage and having babies. He'd told her that was never going to happen.

The last one had been Ingrid, eight months ago or so—a tourist from Norway. She hadn't known who he was. Then some influencer had tagged her out in a bar with 'the son of Iceland's biggest disgrace', and she'd done what Idina had: hightailed it out of town early, blocked him and never spoken to him again. He'd sworn after her there would be no more women.

It was just that Mahlia's quiet spirit and determination, mixed with her vulnerability, had woken something up inside him—something he'd been holding back for far too long. He'd felt it that night at his cabin with her, boiling up and bursting through every pore. It was as if she had taken a hammer to the walls he'd constructed, and he still wasn't exactly sure what to do with that.

Demus had seen it too.

'You like her! And she seems great,' he'd enthused, when he'd carried him inside to the couch. *'It's all on you now, brother. No need to thank me...just don't mess up your chance.'*

He'd messed it up on purpose. She wanted kids—badly, by the sounds of it, and he did not. And his reputation preceded him. There was no way he'd play any part in Mahlia getting ridiculed or slandered. She'd been through enough.

The engine roared in the snow-filled sky, and soon enough Hvítaeyri came into view. 'You can see how blocked the roads are,' he told them, pointing to the mile-high snowdrifts where the cross-section was in summer.

'I hope we can reach her on foot once we're down there,' Mahlia said as Erik relayed to Sven which house they needed to head for.

Gunnar got to his feet and started strapping on his harness.

'There's no way I can land,' came Sven's voice over the headset. 'You're going to have to go down on the winch, Gunnar.'

'Already on it,' he confirmed.

'Helga's contractions are getting closer together,' Erik followed up.

He'd been talking with whoever was with the woman in labour the whole way here, and it was clear Mahlia was taking mental notes. Gunnar had no doubt she could deliver that baby on her own if she had to. Was there anything she couldn't do? he mused, pulling his line tighter around his middle. How her ex could have tried to repress her in any way made him want to hunt him down in the chopper and throw a live alligator at him from the winch.

'I'm ready for you,' he told her.

Mahlia stood up, meeting his eyes with fierce resolve. He hooked up the winch line to his harness and then secured it around her slim waist, making sure she was safely attached to him. Now they were strapped together, their next movements were vital. She was his responsibility on this wire—it was up to him to ensure she got down there in one piece.

He checked all the connections twice before giving a nod of approval. Mahlia took long, deep breaths as she followed him closer to the chopper door, now open wide onto an abyss of white. Maybe he was attuned to her now, but he was sure he could feel her trepidation radiating outwards, despite her brave face. She was obviously wary of jumping in this weather.

'I'll be with you,' he said against her ear, as her hair sprang free and tickled his cheeks. Her natural, musky, womanly scent had him struggling to resist the urge to take her hands, but he gave her an encouraging pat on the shoulder in front of the others, and she leaned in, eyes on his. 'We can do this,' he said. 'Just keep your eyes on me.'

Ásta and Erik were watching, offering words of encouragement, double-checking that Mahlia's radio was strapped on and the backpack was tight on her back over the harness. The cold wind seemed to howl louder as they edged further towards the door. Below them, villagers had gathered, cheering them on, some dragging sledges loaded with supplies.

Mahlia locked her gaze onto his. 'I'm OK, I trust you,' she told him.

So he stepped with her off the ledge.

Soon, the rotors' thumping, deafening noise was metres above them as they were lowered slowly to the ground, swaying in the wind. He didn't need to feel the cable—he knew from memory it was secure, with or without him holding it. He felt Mahlia's gloved hands wrap tightly around his, watched her look around her in awe as she dangled, suspended with him, her hips pressed to his in the air.

Not kissing her suddenly took every ounce of restraint in his body.

On the ground, Gunnar quickly unhooked Mahlia from his harness. The chopper would circle, but if the snow picked up they'd have to head back without them and return later. It was just him and Mahlia now.

'This way—Helga lives down here,' someone told them, pointing down a street with snow-drifts so high at the sides they could barely see the buildings.

'Give me the backpack,' he told Mahlia, but she refused.

'It's not heavy,' she told him, beckoning him to follow her as she strode on ahead, with a crowd of people eager to be involved.

'Fine,' he responded to himself, suppressing a smile.

With heavy snowfall covering most of the houses in sight, and a thick blanket of fog rolling off the mountainside, they trudged through several streets. They would have identified which house it was without any help, he thought. The cries of pain coming from inside were impossible to miss.

Mahlia rushed indoors to the woman's side and stood by her bed, shrugging off the backpack. Helga was groaning in pain, a nightdress heaved up around her thighs under a thick blanket.

'Helga,' she said, taking her hand. 'I understand your contractions are coming quickly... I'm a paramedic, and I'm here to help. My name is Mahlia.'

'They're coming so fast, I can't...'

Helga squeezed her blue eyes shut, clutched her bump. Then let out the most agonising wail that ricocheted around the room and might have started an avalanche somewhere outside.

Mahlia quickly took stock of the situation. The sheer curtains were drawn closed over the small window above a dresser loaded with animal ornaments. The only light came from the fireplace in the corner, where flickering red flames threw shadows across the room.

'Gunnar, open the curtains,' she instructed him, pulling off her coat and draping it over an upholstered chair in the corner.

They needed all the light they could get.

Although Helga's contractions were coming quickly, she was not yet fully dilated. Still, it was too late to try and transport her anywhere else. She and Gunnar were going to have to deliver this baby themselves.

A gruff, burly, red-faced man appeared holding one hand out. He stopped Gunnar in his tracks halfway to the window. 'Not you. I don't want you near my daughter.'

Mahlia hurried back to them as Helga huffed and puffed on the bed. 'What's the problem?' she asked calmly, throwing her scarf on top of her coat. She assumed this man was Helga's father—someone else who had an issue with Gunnar. She noticed his leathery hands, gnarled with scars.

'I know who you are,' the man said gruffly, still looking threateningly at Gunnar. His cheeks were ruddy, his eyes watery and bloodshot, as if he'd been up all night. 'Your father helped bring my fishing business to its knees, Gunnar Johansson, and we lost *all* our foreign buyers. It took us years to turn a profit again, and we're still not back to how it was before...'

'Gunnar is *not* his father—and now is not the time for this.'

Mahlia's authoritative tone shocked even herself. She caught the surprise and admiration in Gunnar's eyes, just as Helga let out another shriek behind them.

Mahlia raced to the curtains herself, flung them open, then hurried back to the bedside. 'Gunnar, can you find us some warm, dry towels?'

Gunnar, still dripping snow from his boots onto the wooden floor, moved to pass the angry man—only to be stopped again.

'Sir!' Mahlia called out, furious now. 'With all due respect, this man got up at five a.m., drove through a blizzard, and has just lowered himself *and* me on a wire from a helicopter to help your daughter. Are you really going to stand in his way?'

'Daddy!'

Helga's scream of agony stunned the man into silence. He staggered back against the wall, finally letting Gunnar pass.

Mahlia heard a woman in the hallway with him, hopefully getting them some towels. Her heart was pounding. This was not what she'd expected when she'd woken up this morning, but at least Gunnar was here, and had been allowed back in the room.

Thankfully the antagonistic father kept away as she encouraged poor Helga through another wave of pain. Her bedsheets were soaked in sweat now. She was shaking from the pain of her contractions. Gunnar squeezed her hand and kept passing warm towels, counting between contractions, monitoring her blood pressure, while Mahlia checked for a crowning head, reminding her to take deep breaths.

'You can do this, Helga,' she soothed.

'You're almost there,' Gunnar encouraged, handing her the Entonox mask, which she grabbed and pressed to her mouth for dear life.

Her face seemed both pale and flushed in the firelight, and her eyes were tightly closed as she drew breaths through clenched teeth, then the mask, then her teeth again.

'Almost there,' Mahlia repeated.

Helga writhed in pain. She was panting faster and faster, her grip tight on Gunnar's hand. When he met Mahlia's eyes in the firelight a flush of gratitude for his silent strength made her smile at him and mouth *Thank you*.

His silent strength and approachability were exactly the things that had kept her talking the other night—more than the moonshine had. She didn't care what his father had done...but she did care how it affected him and his family, she realised. He *wasn't* his father; he was a good man.

As far as you know, a little voice tinkled in her head.

She didn't want any reason to doubt that—not after what she'd been through with Javid. That was the real reason she wasn't reading the rest of the stuff about Gunnar on the Internet, the gossip and slander. She didn't want to wonder if any of it might be true.

Learning something she *didn't* like about this man would prove Javid right: that she was a terrible judge of character, too trusting, too naive, unworthy of the career she'd built and the dreams she'd dared to share and put into action. But some of those ideas *were* worthy—like the e-assist bikes. With Demus on the trial she could bring some light to his life while she was here, and to Gunnar's by association. And after she was gone they'd *still* have that.

'He's coming…he's coming!' Helga winced, before emitting the biggest scream yet.

The baby's head was crowning. Mahlia urged Helga on, and so did Gunnar. His hand had turned white in the young woman's grip. Then a little head appeared between Helga's legs, followed by two tiny shoulders.

'He's here!' she told them excitedly, and a within minutes a beautiful baby boy had slipped out into the waiting towel in Mahlia's hands.

'Well done, Helga, you have a son.'

Gunnar checked the baby over—ten toes, ten fingers, a cute button nose. Mahlia watched the way he held him like a precious treasure, so tiny in his massive hands. When he caught her watching he seemed to hurry up. He snipped the cord like a pro, and she handed the warm bundle to a sobbing, relieved Helga.

'He's beautiful and healthy,' she told her.

'He's Magnús.' Helga sniffed, beaming through her tears. 'Oh, Magnús, you look just like your daddy. He's on his way to meet you, I promise. He's just stuck in the snow.'

Hearing the name, and the reason why Helga's partner wasn't there, made tears spring unexpectedly into Mahlia's own eyes. She was exhausted, but outside the snow was coming down thick and fast again. The helicopter wouldn't be able to land…maybe not for hours. Days?

She started picking up the towels, wondering how they were supposed to get out of here without going back up on the winch, just as Helga's father broke away and stuck his hand out to Gunnar.

'Sorry about what I said before,' he told him, somewhat reluctantly. 'I shouldn't have judged you without knowing you. We couldn't have done this without you.'

Mahlia fought to hide the smug look on her face as Gunnar accepted his apology. Then he threw her a slightly sheepish, pleased grin that made her heart soar like an eagle in her chest.

The two of them walked in silence in the snow to a tiny café bar. It was more like a shed, and almost empty. Snowdrifts blocked the windows, but the place was fire-lit and welcoming, and only three doors down from Helga in case she needed them while they waited for news from the team.

Gunnar placed two cups of coffee down on a rickety old table and took the seat opposite her. She excused herself to use the bathroom, and on her return, before she could take her seat again, he scraped his chair back loudly. Before she knew what was what, he'd swept her up against him into a giant embrace.

'Thank you,' he said into her hair.

His arms wrapped around her and his warmth seeped through his clothes into hers, into her skin.

'What for?' she asked him, wiping at her eyes against his shoulder.

It had been a long time since a man had swept her up into a hug—one so solid and protective and sincere. She breathed into it, committing the tender moment to memory. It was like wearing his sweater, but better.

'For what you did in there. And for saying what you said to Helga's father. You didn't have to.'

'Yes, I did.'

She let her arms fall around his shoulders for a moment, relishing the bulk of his muscular frame against her small one and his words. He really did think she was special. They were pretty special as a team too. And there was no point denying the way her heart had almost escaped through her mouth onto his lips when she'd been harnessed to him on the winch earlier. There was something between them, but was it a good idea to explore it or not? She needed to know what had happened the other night to make him pull back. Suddenly there were lots of things she needed to know, for her own peace of mind.

Releasing herself, she slid back into her seat. 'The other night, in the hot tub, I thought you were going to kiss me,' she said, with a nervous laugh.

Gunnar's mouth became a thin line as he averted his eyes. 'That wasn't why I invited you out there, Mahlia.'

She sat back, blinking. 'I didn't think it was.'

'Well, you're married. People talk. We shouldn't…'

His eyes darted around the room now, as if he was suddenly worried someone might have seen their embrace. No one was looking. It was only them and the barman here, and he was out at the back.

'But you did,' she pressed. 'You did almost kiss me, despite all that.'

His mouth twitched. 'Maybe I chickened out. For numerous reasons.'

'It sounds like you were counting a lot of reasons *not* to kiss me, Gunnar.'

'Did you want me to, then?' he tested.

She shut her mouth as her pulse quickened. Already she had no clue where she was getting the courage to say all this to him. He went through women like hotcakes, apparently. But maybe part of her wanted to be one of them. Maybe she wanted something hot, fast, delicious, to remind her that she could be desirable. She'd been far too scared to do much at all with Javid, in the end, stuck in her shell. No way was she ever going to be that person again.

'Did I want you to kiss me?' she mused aloud, stirring her coffee with a shiny teaspoon. 'I did and I didn't. I was confused Javid was bugging me, and you and Demus were being so nice. And...'

'Moonshine,' they said at the same time.

She dragged a hand through her hair, realising it was tangled from their windy descent on the winch. 'I just wanted to know more about you, Gunnar. From you.'

'Well, now you know,' he replied stoically, stroking a hand across his chin and letting out a sigh. 'That guy has a right to be upset with my family. My father ruined so many people's lives.'

She tutted at him. 'He didn't do it on his own. And *you* had nothing to do with it.'

He sipped his coffee, frowning. 'Not directly, I guess, no.'

'So why are you letting yourself think that somehow you're the bad guy?'

'It's what *everyone* thinks.'

'Not everyone,' she told him sternly. 'Your brother adores you. I like what you guys have together. I'm jealous, actually.'

He curled his fingers into his palms. 'You don't have any siblings?'

'Nope. Mum and Dad always seemed pretty happy with just me. Mind you, they weren't around a whole lot. Mum was a scientist—a botanist. She spent all her time in the lab until she retired. Dad used to joke how she would've rather married him in a white lab coat instead of a dress, and honeymooned in the greenhouse if he'd let her.'

Gunnar smiled a shadow of a smile. It boosted her to keep talking.

'Dad's an art historian. He started lecturing at the local university when I was a kid. So they were probably too busy to have any more children.'

He looked at her thoughtfully, and she found herself considering for the first time how maybe she'd been seeking attention from Javid, and done her best to always please him, because she hadn't had much attention from her parents growing up. While they'd loved her, they certainly hadn't seemed too pleased when she'd been hanging around in the school holidays, taking up space and time. And in later years, following her aunt's death, depression had gripped her grieving mother so hard it had forced up a wall between them all.

'But you want children of your own?' he said slowly.

Mahlia blinked. What was he getting at? He knew the answer to that, didn't he? Something told her he wasn't one to forget. Somehow it felt like a test.

'I did… I do. I know I have a few trust issues, after what's happened. And I also know my age could be a factor… But there are ways. I've already thought about how I might do it,' she admitted in a rush.

She needed to feel needed. Always had done. Kids would give her a new purpose, as much as her career was giving her one now. She'd never doubted it.

Gunnar was nodding quietly. She caught his eyes and he looked away quickly.

'How did you meet Javid?' he asked.

'We reached for the same loaf of bread at the bakery,' she told him over her coffee cup. 'It was the last one. I let him have it.'

Of course she'd let him have it. And he'd taken it, too.

'He asked me out and that was it, really. I know now we had nothing in common.'

'So why did you like him initially?'

Mahlia stared at him. Somehow she was thinking about his sweater, still folded up on her bed in her apartment. It had felt so comfortable on her, in a way nothing of Javid's ever had. Maybe that was why she hadn't given it back yet, she thought, guiltily.

'I don't know. He was…different.'

Different meaning he'd seemed like a dependable choice compared to all the losers she'd seemed to meet online, she thought. He'd arranged their dates and hadn't ever cancelled.

'Why did you like Idina?' she asked.

Gunnar was silent for a moment, as if pondering the question. 'She was tough. She was really into sports. She encouraged me to pursue my goals. She was…like me, I guess. We had a best friend type of vibe. Best friends with benefits. We just *liked* each other.'

And that's the difference, Mahlia thought to herself, feeling envy seep like poison through her pores. That was why Gunnar had loved Idina and been so hurt by her abandonment.

She was here in Iceland trying to distance herself as much as possible from Javid. They'd never been friends, she and Javid. She'd never really even *liked* him. She had settled for the first man who'd shown an ounce of commitment, then turned herself into his puppet.

Gunnar's radio sprang into life. It was as they'd feared. There was no way out for a least a few hours. A team was still working on clearing the road back to Reykjavik and it was too dangerous to bring the chopper back in.

'What do people do in tiny mountain villages when there's a blizzard raging outside?' she asked him, staring at the relentless snowflakes, just as the barman came over and told them the coffee was on the house. He'd heard what they'd done for Helga.

Gunnar looked surprised. He always seemed surprised when someone was nice to him.

The two men exchanged a few words in Icelandic, before he turned to her: 'Looks like we have an invitation.'

'To what?' she asked.

'You want to see what Icelanders do when there's a blizzard raging outside?'

CHAPTER EIGHT

THE SMALL ONE-LEVEL house was half hidden by snowdrifts, like most of the homes in the village. Mahlia followed Gunnar up the pathway, which had clearly been dug out by hand.

He stopped by the door for a minute, casting her a look. 'I don't usually do this, but the guy in the café said they're expecting us.'

'Who?' she asked, intrigued.

'The villagers.'

Sinister giant icicles glistened ominously from the low roof above the windows, threatening to fall and pierce whatever they struck, and she felt his apprehension. He was probably thinking there'd be at least someone in there who wouldn't want him around, but he was doing this for her.

She touched his hand through his glove. 'We don't have to…'

Too late. The door was flung open.

Lively Icelandic voices assaulted her ears as a beaming, red-faced woman in her sixties ushered them inside. It was toasty warm.

'A party?' Mahlia looked up at Gunnar in surprise.

'People in small villages take it in turns to host nights like this—especially when the weather's bad,' he told her, unzipping his coat, holding his hand out for hers, still looking around warily. 'Which is most of the time. Everyone brings a dish. Everyone can play.'

'Play what?' she asked, just as a piano sprang to life.

A tall, striking middle-aged man in a vivid red and blue sweater was playing something jovial she didn't recognise, but it reminded her of Christmas parties back when she'd actually gone out with her friends. At least five more people instantly gathered around it and started singing. Everyone had a glass of something—probably alcohol. From what she'd learned so far about Icelanders, they loved to drink.

'Gunnar, this is so nice!'

The scent of cinnamon and nutmeg filled the air. Evergreen branches were strung up by the windows, illuminated by twinkling lights and candles. There must be about twenty-five people here. Not one of them was looking at Gunnar the way Helga's father had. In fact they came over one by one, introduced themselves, thanked them for being here. She felt like a minor celebrity.

'Help yourself to food,' their hostess said

warmly, taking their coats and directing Gunnar to leave their bags in an adjacent room. 'Ólafur told me you delivered Helga's son today. You're our guests tonight—we're really grateful you could make it.'

Mahlia hadn't realised how hungry she was until she was standing at a large buffet table. Her stomach growled as she took in the array of food. Smoked salmon sandwiches, glazed ham, giant meatballs, pickled herring, intricate pastries and gingerbread cookies shaped like stars and hearts. *Delicious.*

Gunnar popped a tiny sandwich into his mouth whole, just as Helga's father emerged from what she assumed was the bathroom and spotted him.

'Here he is!' he exclaimed, lunging forward like a hulking barrel and aiming for a one-armed hug.

Gunnar accepted it awkwardly.

'How is Helga? How's the baby?' Mahlia asked him.

'They're wonderful…just wonderful,' he proclaimed, releasing Gunnar. 'Sleeping now.'

'That's great.' She smiled around her cookie, which was the best cookie she'd ever tasted.

'Everybody, this is Gunnar Johansson! All is forgiven—right, my friend?' He paused, screwing up his nose. 'Well, you. Not your father. If Ingólfur Johansson was here I'd…'

'Not now, Sigurður,' their hostess said, throwing them both an apologetic look.

She led the man away, to the piano. Gunnar looked astonished, to say the least. Helga's father was clearly about five drinks in already.

'Drink?' Gunnar asked her, pouring himself one from a decanter on the table.

She shook her head. There was no way she was ever drinking around Gunnar again; the effects of this homemade Icelandic stuff were unpredictable, to say the least.

This group of Icelanders turned out to be incredibly talented. Gunnar was right—everyone seemed to be able to play an instrument. There were guitars, a flute, a violin, even a tambourine.

It had been years since Mahlia had played the guitar. Javid had laughed at her the last time she'd picked hers up...told her not to give up her day job.

She sipped on mint tea and sneaked glances at Gunnar when he wasn't looking. He seemed to be relaxing, chatting to people with ease. She couldn't help wondering what he'd been thinking earlier, when he'd held that baby. There had been a look on his face then that she hadn't been able to read. Maybe he wanted a family someday, she thought idly, not for the first time. He'd be a good dad, someone like him, a leader...

Why are you even thinking about this?

She rolled her eyes, just as her phone chimed in her pocket. Pulling it out in surprise she stared at it. There hadn't been a signal till now. Her heart lurched. Javid.

Are you ever going to talk to me again? I'm worried about you. Are you OK? How can you just ignore me like this, Mahlia? It's so heartless!

She ground her teeth, scowling at the screen. Ever since she'd ignored him on her birthday she'd kept it up. It was the longest she'd gone without pandering to his needs in seven years. She'd felt pretty powerful at first...at times had even forgotten about him!

'What's happened?' Gunnar asked.

He was standing in front of her now, frowning.

'Nothing.' She shoved the phone away, feeling stupid. Of course he probably thought she was silly for not just blocking his number altogether.

'I've got a signal too,' he said, holding up his phone. 'My mother's in trouble again.'

He didn't sound pleased.

'What?'

'Nothing you need to get in involved in,' he grunted.

She watched his brow crease harder. The shadow of stubble on his cheeks and chin gave him more of a Viking aura than ever.

A woman took the piano stool behind him; everyone started singing.

'I don't think we'll be getting out of here any time soon, though. Not tonight, anyway. We've been offered two rooms at the guesthouse.'

'OK…' she said, wondering what was up with his mother.

He'd been pretty vague about her so far. It was none of her business, of course, and she simmered in silence, berating herself for wanting to know anyway. He was already taking up far too much of her headspace. First Javid, now him.

Scrolling through her emails quickly, for anything she might have missed today, she spotted a message from Inka. She was back from Spain and keen to get the trial moving—and, yes, of *course* she'd like Demus Johansson to be involved.

'She calls him "high-profile",' she told Gunnar. 'Is that a good thing or a bad thing?'

'What do you think?' he replied, folding his arms, propping up the wall. 'He'll do your trial, but he probably won't want to do any press around the bikes.'

Mahlia chewed on her lip, focused on the tapestries on the wall behind him. It hadn't really crossed her mind that Demus would be wary of the media, but she knew Gunnar was right; she'd seen the way it had treated the family when she'd briefly looked up Gunnar on the Internet.

Gunnar looked as if he was somewhere else in his head. Thinking about his mother, maybe? What was going on?

A huge cheer erupted as the pianist finished her song. 'Anyone else? Our special guests, maybe?'

Everyone turned to look at them in anticipation. Gunnar shook his head, still lost in his thoughts. Mahlia felt rude, not getting involved, standing over here with Gunnar, reading messages, while everyone was being so hospitable. Should she play? It had been years…and Javid had said she was bad at it…

Oh, stuff Javid.

Before she could chicken out, she strode to the piano, picked up a guitar from its stand and dropped to the stool. She ran her fingers over the strings, feeling the familiar vibrations of the instrument against her skin. Her mind raced, trying to remember the chords of a song she'd used to play in high school.

How did it go?

Oh, yes.

Mahlia began to strum, and each chord swept her further into the music. It was like visiting a house she hadn't seen in years, remembering every nook and corner.

The crowd soon recognised the song. Helga's

father started singing along in his thick, deep baritone. Others followed, and Mahlia couldn't keep the smile from her face as Gunnar took his place beside her on the piano stool.

To her total shock, he started accompanying her on the keys. Their harmonies cascaded through the room, his fingers flying like a master musician. She watched him in awe, picking at the guitar strings beside him. Wow. He was so talented!

All around them hands were clapping, voices joined in harmony. She hadn't felt this sense of togetherness in a room in years…maybe not ever. As they hit the final notes the cheers and applause turned deafening, and she realised she was shaking with adrenaline. She turned to Gunnar. His bad mood had dissipated somewhere between the piano keys. She met his huge smile face-on, and before she could stop herself her body reacted to the moment.

She leaned forward over the guitar and kissed him on the cheek. 'You were so good,' she whispered, laughing with the shock of her own actions.

'*Me?* You were…'

For a moment Gunnar looked just as he had that night in the hot tub. She held her breath. His gaze moved over her face, lingering on her lips till his smile faded. The intensity of his eyes burned into her.

But in a beat, he was on his feet. She watched in horror as the stool scraped out from under her and Gunnar snatched someone's phone from their hands.

'No photos,' he barked, sending the crowd silent.

He apologised straight away, keeping his voice calm enough, but he was visibly annoyed. 'Please, guys, no photos. That's all I ask.'

Mahlia felt sick, and angry. But mostly sick. The girl apologised profusely, and Gunnar told her it was fine, but the moment was ruined. She hadn't even seen anyone taking photos!

'Why is it such a big deal if they take a photo?' she asked, her tone rising as he guided her towards the hallway. His hand was only resting lightly against the small of her back now, but his intent was clearly to leave. To urge her out of a moment she'd been enjoying.

'Gunnar, don't be so…domineering!'

'We should go,' he said, gathering up their coats.

He fetched their bags while her mind spun.

'I don't want to go,' she said, glowering at him.

This was all too familiar; she couldn't even count on a thousand people's fingers how many times Javid had forced her to leave somewhere she'd been having a good time.

'*You* go. I'm staying here.'

Her words hung heavy between them, daring him to challenge her. Inside her chest her heart beat a frantic tempo, faster than whoever was now on the guitar. Every nerve-ending bristled as she waited for his response. She watched his face change, his eyes narrow, the faintest twitch of his lips.

'I'm sorry,' he said after a moment, swiping up his stuff. 'You stay as long as you want. The guesthouse is just up the street.' He turned his back on her, making for the door. 'I'll see you tomorrow, Mahlia. Have fun.'

Wait... What?

She watched in disbelief as he left.

Staring at the door, she half expected him to open it again and demand she leave with him, but it stayed closed.

Really?

He hadn't argued or pushed or tried to make her do something she didn't want to—he'd just apologised and agreed with her.

Warmth flooded through her body—so much so she found herself laughing behind her hand as she turned back to the party. They were all dancing now, pulling her in as if they were old friends, telling her how great she was on the guitar. Gunnar's reaction to the phone camera was clean forgotten. Javid was forgotten.

She joined in with the dancing, let her hair flow down around her shoulders, felt her hips loosen and her worries fall away. She forgot the blizzard outside…forgot everything. In this one moment she felt more powerful than she'd ever felt before.

Gunnar balled his fists at his sides, pacing the tiny room. There was only just enough space in here for the bed and a rather old, shabby-looking couch that had seen better days. He'd be sleeping on it as soon as Mahlia got back.

There'd been some mix-up. The guy who'd let him in had rushed off somewhere afterwards but Gunnar had only been able to find one unlocked room in the place. Now there was no one around to ask for another.

He stopped at the window to look for her through the falling snow for what must have been the hundredth time. He'd locked the door downstairs against the snow and wind, so he'd have to let her in when she returned, but she'd been gone for three hours. The message he'd sent her about the room-sharing situation was still unread. Maybe he should go and check she was OK.

No.

She'd made it more than clear she didn't need

him there. These gatherings went on all night sometimes, especially in weather like this, and he was still kicking himself for reacting that way to the girl and her phone... No wonder Mahlia was annoyed. He'd tried to get her to leave! He'd probably reminded her of her awful ex.

Gunnar sank to the bed, pressed his palms over his eyes and yawned. It turned into a growl. God knew that idiot Javid was controlling enough; the last thing Mahlia needed was for *him* to start acting so... What was it she'd called him? *Domineering.* It was just that the thought of a photo like that getting out...of them in a situation like that... She didn't know the storm it would cause for her, being linked to him. He was flirting with danger enough, being seen with her anywhere that wasn't work-related, and now this.

A buzz came from his phone. He grabbed for it, expecting it to be her. It was Demus. Quickly, he answered. 'It's the middle of the night...are you all right, bud?'

'Ma finally passed out in her bed. I just got back to my place. I figured you'd still be at that party.'

Gunnar walked to the window again, telling him he was alone for the moment. 'I'm so sorry you had to deal with all that by yourself. Was your carer OK to stay with you while you rescued Ma? Did she help you run the bath for her?'

He watched for any sign of Mahlia through the howling wind and snow, biting the inside of his cheek as Demus filled him in on the latest. Ma had got herself so drunk that she'd locked herself out of her house. Failing to reach him, she had called Demus. Demus and whichever one of his carers had been there with him at the time had then had to undertake the hellish mission to go out in the snow with the spare key and locate her in the backyard, where she probably would have frozen to death if she hadn't been so loaded on vodka.

'Any news on when you'll be back yet?' Demus asked.

'Tomorrow. They're clearing the road as we speak.'

Demus sighed, his voice tight. 'We need to do something about Ma, Gunnar. It's getting out of control…it can't go on like this.'

'I know,' he said gruffly. Just hearing his brother so weary made him angry; he wasn't supposed to be dealing with any of this. 'Maybe it's time for rehab.'

'She won't go—you know that. She wants to be home in case Dad comes back.'

He gritted his teeth. God, every time they talked about this he fought a tidal wave of shame and anger and loathing for his father that felt so toxic he wanted to vomit.

His eyes fell to a figure beneath the window, huddled against the snow. *Mahlia*.

'Demus, I'll call you tomorrow. Get some rest.'

He met her at the door, before she could press the buzzer—there was still no one else here to let her in.

She almost stumbled into him in surprise. 'Gunnar. How come you're still awake?'

He ushered her inside, shutting the door against the snow.

Mahlia studied his face and her eyes darkened. 'What's wrong? You're still worried about your mother?'

He almost laughed. He'd been expecting her to be angry with him, but instead she was asking about his mother. She seemed to sense his internal stress, as if she was peering into his very soul.

'Gunnar?'

He scraped his hands through his hair, so as not to touch her. 'Can you forgive me for acting like I did back there? I should *never* have tried to make you leave. I had no right.'

Snowflakes glistened in her hair as she smiled. 'I had the best time,' she said, eyes shining. 'You have no idea. And you didn't make me do anything.'

He frowned. 'I tried, though. Then I just... left you there.'

She laughed. 'Exactly—it was perfect!'

Maybe it was the conversation with Demus, or maybe it was his own shame over his reaction earlier, but he was just so happy to see her face, free from any anger and resentment, that it was all he could do not to draw her into him and never let her go.

Instead he led her up the stairs, told her about the mix-up with the rooms, said that he'd take the couch. She eyed him cautiously as she took off her coat and pulled off her shoes, and he forced a smile into his voice, pulling off his sweater, hoping he was hiding his inner turmoil.

'If this is a little awkward I can…'

'What? Sleep in the hall? Take the bed,' she told him.

He stopped halfway through unbuttoning his shirt. 'No way.'

Mahlia's gaze fell to his chest. Then she tore it away. 'I'm smaller than you. The couch is fine for me. I'm so tired, I could probably sleep in the bathtub.'

He grunted, pulling off his shoes, watching the way she looked at his feet in his socks, then averted her eyes again.

'We'll leave sleeping in bathtubs to my mother,' he said, before he could think.

She dropped to the couch as he pulled some

spare blankets from a cupboard. 'What happened? Talk to me.'

'I don't want to talk about it,' he said. Why drag her into it? She didn't need to be involved. 'Everything's good.'

'It's not good,' she insisted.

'It's *good*,' he repeated.

She was biting back a smile now. 'You know, you were really *good* on that piano. I wish you could've stayed longer.'

He crawled under the down quilt on the bed, trying not to watch as she shrugged out of her sweater and huddled under the blankets on the couch. This was torture, just as he'd known it would be.

Suppressing a groan, he told her she was pretty incredible on the guitar too, leaving out the word *sexy*, even though she'd looked sexy as hell playing that thing.

'It's probably not a good idea for us to do anything like that again, Mahlia,' he said instead, willing his heart to stop crashing through his ribs. 'If you knew what kind of reputation me and my family have…just being seen with me could…'

She clicked her tongue. 'Oh, so *that's* why you didn't want a photo! Gunnar, your family legacy doesn't have to end with what your dad did. And I'm a big girl. I can look after my—'

A creak from the couch made her close her mouth. Before Mahlia could even stand up, a shuddering splitting sound tore through the room, and the couch broke clean in half. She sat there swallowed by cushions, on the broken frame, stunned, mouth agape. Gunnar stared in horror, too shocked to move.

'Oh, my...'

He couldn't help it. He started to laugh—a huge belly laugh that shook him and pushed every negative thought he'd been thinking straight from his head. It was just too funny.

Her face was mask of disbelief as she surveyed the wreckage around her, mortified. 'How did that even happen?'

'It looks ancient,' he told her.

He slipped off the bed and helped her to her bare feet. She was shorter without shoes. Her toenails were painted a deep green, he noted, running his eyes back up to hers. Carefully he reached for a piece of stuffing in her hair.

'How do you always do this?' he murmured as she froze in his gaze.

'Break ancient couches?' Her voice was a whisper now; neither of them were laughing.

'No. Make me want to kiss you.' He stepped closer, reached for her face, tracing her soft, full lips with his thumb. She closed her eyes and swallowed. 'I've been telling myself not to.'

Mahlia's hand came up over his, holding him in place. 'But what if I want you to?'

Every inch of Gunnar's body was alive with desire; it was highly probable he'd never wanted anyone more than he wanted her in this moment. Mahlia's whole face had glazed over with a longing he'd never seen, and in that second it was inevitable.

She went for him, pulling him in, kissing him passionately, till their tongues were tangling and exploring and they were falling back onto the bed, not caring if that broke, too.

Neither of them could pull away for what felt like an eternity. The electricity between them was palpable, heating up the room, sheening their skin. Mahlia's shirt and bra were on the floor by his clothes…her caramel skin and dark curls were on the pillow beneath him… It all felt like a dream in the dim light. The way her lips and hands felt on his mouth, on his body…

Gunnar finally pulled away, looking down at her, his face inches from hers. Her heart was racing like a motor against his chest. Taking a deep breath, he forced himself to roll away, slamming his head back against the pillow. 'If I keep going, I won't be able to stop.'

'I don't want you to stop,' she said.

The need in her voice was agonising and it tore at his soul. She reached out and touched his face gently, before leaning in to kiss him again, this time more slowly and tenderly than before, as if she was pouring her heart into him. How was it possible to want her even more? All of her...

'No, Mahlia.'

He forced his feet to the floor and went into the bathroom, determined to shake it off. If he made love to her now, he'd get hooked—and then ruin her life, probably. This had already gone too far.

He kicked off his briefs, turned on the shower, standing there till the water scalded his skin. What the hell was wrong with him? He'd only hurt her... And worse, selfishly, he'd be the one left missing what might have been when she disappeared.

You said you'd never do this to yourself again!

'It's just one night,' came a voice from behind him.

He spun around. Mahlia was stepping out of her black cotton panties. They were already damp—he'd felt them, felt *her*, enough to know that if they didn't do this now it would torture them both. But he would *not* do this—to either of them.

'I'm not good for you,' he groaned as she walked towards him slowly.

He stood under the water, paralysed by the full sight of her, sculpted arms, shapely legs,

hips, breasts, curves…the most beautiful creature he'd ever seen. Oh, God, why did she have
to be so perfect?

'Mahlia, I'm warning you.'

'I'm not asking you to be good,' she told him,
stepping into the cubicle, pressing herself up
against him, sucking softly on his shoulder. Her
soft skin glistened under the spray as he moaned,
feeling every last ounce of resolve wash down
the plughole. He surrendered, let her take control of him. What else could he do?

She wanted it, she wanted to feel powerful, and he'd never been so turned on by anyone. When she got down on her knees under
the pouring water he ran his hands through her
hair, watching the water running over the curve
of her shoulders, and blanked everything else
from his mind.

CHAPTER NINE

'THAT WAS SO much better than I ever expected,' Mahlia found herself saying in disbelief. 'I never thought I'd be so emotional about this…sorry.'

Standing in the wind, she ran a hand across her eyes and her jaw in disbelief as Demus sped over the line on the trial circuit, faster than he'd done it the first time.

Gunnar boomed, 'Yes!' thumping the sky with his fist, and Inka clapped her hands together in delight, along with the other participants all waiting their turn.

'That's even faster than I did it,' Inka squealed, high-fiving Mahlia from her wheelchair beside her. 'Thirty-two miles per hour.' She looked between her and Gunnar in disbelief. 'On this terrain that's pretty much…'

'A miracle?' Gunnar said, finishing Inka's words.

Inka made her way over to greet Demus with a huge grin on her face, no doubt to check the gadget on the bike was functioning correctly.

It fed data to an app on her phone—something else Mahlia had been working with a developer to perfect.

'I never I thought I'd see it. Maybe this means we can finally ride together again, out there.'

Gunnar waved a hand out to the mountains beyond the covered trial circuit. His blue eyes were flooded with such pure, childlike joy she couldn't help a laugh bubbling up.

He wrapped his arms around her waist suddenly and pulled her close, pressing a searing kiss to her forehead that seemed to burn with an intensity of its own. Instantly she was shot like a bullet in reverse, back to the first night they'd made love. Seven amazing, unforgettable nights ago. They'd spent most nights together since, but that first time...

When they'd finished making love in the shower, and on the bed, the clock had read six a.m., and neither of them had slept at all. That had been the first time in a long time she'd felt in control like that, she thought, swallowing the lump that built up in her throat every time she recalled the intensity of their lovemaking.

'I'm not good for you.'

The way he'd said it, like a warning, hadn't stopped her. If anything, it had spurred her on. Every whisper of a touch on her skin, every growl against her mouth with the snow flying around outside…it had all driven her deeper into his eyes and his arms and made her burn to feel him deeper inside her.

He released her now, seeming to remember they weren't alone. She buzzed from his heat, even in the freezing weather.

In that moment, after dancing all night at that party, her confidence had shot through the snow-topped roof. *Now or never*, the voice in her head had encouraged, the second she'd stepped into that bathroom and seen him in all his glory, standing like a Viking with the water cascading off his broad shoulders, over his firm abs.

Eventually Javid had appalled her so much that sex with him had come to feel like a performance, a duty—something to get over with as fast as possible, then wash off. Now she knew sex could be so vastly different, it was near impossible not to want it to happen again and again with Gunnar. He touched her in a way that sent her mind spinning away from her and left her body tingling from her fingertips to her toes.

Addictive, she thought, as Demus took off on the track again. Yes, they'd meant to stop after one delicious night, but the sex had been so amazing they'd just continued. Why talk about where it was going, or when it would inevitably have to end? Why not just live in the moment and enjoy it?

Gunnar hadn't been able to resist her either. In the kitchen of his penthouse apartment, on the rug on the floor of her rental, in the bathroom at the hangar before the others had arrived for a rescue mission last night. No one had any idea.

'This is so great for him,' Gunnar enthused, releasing her. 'Do you know what you've done here, Mahlia? It's life-changing.'

'I've hardly done it alone—but, yes, that was my intention.'

Her heart soared with pride at the thrill of his admiring words—she'd never had anything but negative remarks about her bikes from Javid, and now here she was, watching a successful trial in Iceland, next to Gunnar, who loved what she'd achieved. It was as if she was living in a dream.

Gunnar reached out and softly caressed the skin under her hair for a minute. A bolt of desire went straight to her groin.

'I want to pick you up…take you to that bike shed over there…' he growled against her ear, and she grinned against his cheek.

Then, seeing Inka heading back to them, he pulled away as if she was firing darts from her wheelchair, and put enough space for at least three people between them.

Mahlia bristled, catching her breath. He'd been doing that a lot in public these last few days— reaching for her, making her the centre of their own little universe, then dropping her like a hot potato.

She rubbed her hands together against the cold, focused on what Inka was saying as behind them Demus, his biceps strong from using the chair, transferred himself with ease from the e-bike back to his wheelchair. No, there was no way Javid's low opinions of her worth or sexuality would infiltrate this experience. Gunnar wasn't holding back behind closed doors. Whatever his issues were, even if they stemmed from what his ex had done to him, they were not about her.

But it didn't stop him from keeping her in the dark about some things. Like what was going on with his mother. He still hadn't said what was wrong; it was as if he didn't trust her.

He'd gone to see his mother and Demus at various points all week and hadn't told her anything. She was telling herself she didn't care, that having his body next to hers, having him worship her all night was enough, that it wasn't her business to know everything about him. It wasn't as if they were married!

She still had the tiny issue of getting divorced from Javid to deal with. A formal separation wasn't enough, and a divorce was not something she should be hanging around for, waiting for *him* to decide when he'd sign the papers.

Gunnar excused himself to answer a call without looking at her, and she watched the way his face changed as he spoke. He was worried about something else now. She could literally feel his mood doing a one-eighty.

'What's the matter?' she asked when he returned.

Sure enough, he told her it was nothing for her to worry about—as usual. 'I have to go with Demus now. Are you OK getting back to Reykjavik after the trial?'

She looked around her at the four other participants, chatting amongst themselves, waiting to test out the bike. They only had one prototype here, thanks to some mix-up with the order. The rest would be flown out next week. She'd be at least another couple of hours.

'Where do you have to go? To your mother again?'

His lips tightened as he looked to the floor, and she knew she was right.

'Why won't you tell me anything about what's going on? Maybe I can help.'

'You can't help, Mahlia. And the less you know the better, so you'd do best to stay away,' he almost snapped back.

'*Don't* tell me what's best for me, Gunnar.'

She watched him deflate; he knew he'd struck a nerve.

Good.

'Just let me know you can get back to Reykja-vik on your own,' he said, more gently.

Mahlia's heart thumped in her chest. She straightened, forced the annoyance from her face and voice as best she could, even as she simmered. Now her good mood was ruined too.

'Inka and her carer can take me back.'

'Before you head out, can we get a quick team photo?' Inka said now, coming up to them.

Demus agreed good-naturedly, letting his eyes linger on Inka's profile. Inka noticed and smiled behind her hair. Aha! Was that a spark Mahlia sensed between them? Demus and Inka? How cute!

Gunnar just looked agitated. 'What will the photo be used for?' he asked, checking his phone again.

Inka smiled. 'The Wilderness Association's blog.'

'No social media?'

She told him no, not that she was aware of. Demus rolled his eyes, wheeling over to the others for a line-up, muttering something about Gunnar's extreme paranoia.

Mahlia noticed how Gunnar kept his distance from her even more obviously once the cameras were out, and something inside her shifted irrevocably. Even if she wanted to be linked to him, she couldn't trust that he wouldn't always go out of his way not to link himself to her. He was so ashamed of his family he didn't want her associated with any of it—as if she could care less about *them*! When she was with him she thought she was invincible.

Knowing he was troubled by so many things out of her control made her sadder than it should have. All she cared about was him…all she wanted was his strong arms around her. Which, in essence, should have made her want to run a mile already.

So confusing.

He said his goodbyes, and she watched helplessly as he and Demus's carer loaded his brother into the SUV and drove away.

Mahlia did her best to match Inka's enthusiasm for the rest of the participants. So far all the data looked promising when it came to opening an official e-bike wilderness trail in this area. They'd extend the test circuits to other parks as soon as the snow cleared. Of course she was thrilled it was going so well, but the truth was…

Ugh—where was Gunnar going? Where was he now?

His secrecy was affecting her and overshadowing everything she'd worked for. It was getting more frustrating every time he tried to hide what they were doing, every time he tried to hide what he was doing from her. And it wasn't her place to show it! She wasn't bound to him, and nor was he to her.

So much for being in control of a fling, she thought in despair. She'd stupidly thought it would be a simple hook-up…something to pass the time and boost her confidence…toughen her up so she could give Javid the ultimatum she knew she needed to give him—sign the papers or she'd take it to court. But now Gunnar had her heart in a vicelike grip and she was helpless to break out of it.

This was how it had begun before—how she'd wound up losing herself, she thought. She'd had to keep secrets from Javid. About her needs and her hopes and her friends, her longing for children, to be a mother, to be needed. So much of the last seven years had been about her trying to hide her truth, her*self*…

It was all a lie, pretending she was in control of a casual romance here. Already she was letting someone else overwhelm her emotions.

Not smart, Mahlia. It's been one week, and you're already giddy like a fawn over him. This is going to blow up in your face, one way or another. He is not right for you!

Maybe it was time she ended all this and remembered why she was really here…

* * *

The rescue vehicle rumbled down the dirt track like a thunderstorm, its tyres cutting through the melting ice, sending plumes of water high into the air. Huge puddles collided with the windows like angry tsunamis, threatening to swallow them up as Erik drove on.

'Read me those co-ordinates,' Erik said from the driver's seat, his eyes on the difficult road.

Gunnar complied. 'We're almost at the point they were headed for—they can't be far.'

The Portuguese hikers, a young husband and wife, had gone out of range since making a distress call, and were now somewhere outside the north-eastern corner of Niflheim Valley. A low fog hung over the mountains, which hadn't been the case when the hikers had set out.

Beside him in the back seat, Mahlia was huddled into her hood, her eyes glazed over in thought. She'd been quiet all morning. He had the distinct impression she was annoyed with him and it was obvious why: he'd clammed up on her, as he had a tendency to do when anyone got too close to his business—but what else was he supposed to do?

Just because they were sleeping together, it didn't mean he was about to drag her headfirst from his bed into the Johansson family circus. Besides, this couldn't go anywhere—not really.

Not when she held hopes of starting a family of her own—it would only mean more innocent people to pull down with him.

The image of Ma crying into her dressing gown sleeve wouldn't leave his head. He and Demus had had to sit her down the other day, prise the bottle out of her hands and tell her that if she didn't get professional help and support they wouldn't be available to help her out any more. It broke his heart to think about it, but maybe it would force her to take some damn action.

That photographer had sprung up from no-where when they were on their way out of her house, too, asking when his father was coming home—as if anyone knew! It happened from time to time. Who could tell when another roach would crawl from the woodwork and plaster an-other hyped-up story about Ma, or Demus, or one of his 'flings' all over the Internet? This was *exactly* why he and Demus always made their vis-its to Ma alone.

'Over there!' Mahlia's voice caught him off guard.

'I see it!'

Erik sped up. The car jolted over the deep ruts in the road and her fingers wrapped tighter around her seatbelt, gripping it for dear life, while Gunnar strained his eyes to see what or who they'd spotted.

A lone figure in the distance was scrambling towards them over the snowdrifts. A male, he thought. The husband, whose name was Rodrigo, in a scarlet jacket, flailing his arms in desperation.

Erik veered closer. Mahlia was already out of her seatbelt, poised to open the door. He followed as she burst from the vehicle, snatching up the emergency bag, and he stayed close on her tail as the icy wind whipped through her hair and forced her hood back. He almost yelled at her to let him go first, but knew she'd only ignore him.

Meeting the man halfway, he took in the grizzled beard and haggard face. 'Rodrigo?'

He stumbled as they reached him and collapsed onto the ground. His clothes were soaked through, no doubt from his attempts at wading through the snowbanks to reach help.

'Please…' he begged, his eyes wide with fear.

Mahlia wrapped her own blue scarf around his neck and supported him while he tried to tell them what had happened. Rodrigo's wife Heloísa was back some way, he said. She'd fallen just after she'd started saying she felt sick, and clutching her chest in pain. Panicked, they'd wandered the wrong way back to the path and become lost.

'Don't try and speak any more…just show us

where you left her,' Gunnar told him, putting a hand to Mahlia's elbow as the others caught up with a stretcher and blankets.

Words failed Rodrigo as he convulsed with cold and exhaustion. Soon he was bundled up, and they left him with Erik and Ásta, walking on the way he'd pointed.

Gunnar pulled out his GPS. They ventured deeper into the Niflheim Valley in silence. The snow was coming down through the fog now, thick and treacherous. Icy winds tore at their clothes. But Mahlia trudged on as if he wasn't even there, her face a picture of determination.

He caught her up. 'I know you're mad at me,' he shouted over the wind.

She pursed her lips, but didn't look at him.

'Mahlia,' he persisted. 'You've barely said two words to me for two days!'

'We're not talking about this now.'

'Look, I didn't mean to shut you out,' he continued earnestly as she forged ahead. 'That's the last thing I want to do. There are just…things you don't understand.'

'I'll tell you what I *do* understand,' she said, stopping short in front of him.

Her eyes were gleaming with an unnerving coldness he wasn't used to. It threw him off guard.

'What we've been doing…we shouldn't have

been doing,' she said. 'It was a stupid mistake. You're not good for me, Gunnar. You were totally right about that. And I'm still married.'

It was all he could do not to laugh. 'What are you doing about that, by the way? Have you spoken to him yet? Did you tell him you'll drag his backside through the courts if he doesn't sign the papers?'

She huffed air through her nostrils, gritted her teeth, and he knew the answer. She'd avoided every call he'd seen come in from the guy since they'd met.

'You don't want to talk to him at all? In case he gets an actual hold on you again? In case he makes you go running back to him? Is that it?'

'Give me some credit, Gunnar. I'm not ever going back to him.'

She said it with her brows furrowed and her eyes averted, and he balled his fists. He'd avoided butting in on this topic so far, but now he couldn't hold it in. Her being married was no excuse to end whatever it was they'd kept on doing since that night in Hvítaeyri. She hadn't exactly been acting like someone's wife in *his* bedroom for the last week.

'Then why don't you just have the lawyers do their thing and block his number? Get him out of your life for good?'

'Stop trying to…'

'Trying to *what*, Mahlia?'

'Control what I do!' she spat. 'It's none of your business. We're done, Gunnar.'

He held his hands in the air, forcing his mouth to stay shut as anger pulsed between them.

Done. OK.

This was his fault; he'd kept his business private for her own good, kept them a secret, made sure the whole thing with them existed on *his* terms. That had pushed her buttons, and he could feel the invisible shackles her ex still had her in stretching all the way here from New Zealand. If he ever met this Javid idiot he'd have a real problem not rearranging his face. She might not want to go back to him, but if she didn't cut ties soon...

Not that he should do anything at all—not when he was no more right for her than Javid. She should find someone who wanted the same things she did, he reminded himself. A family!

He spotted something over her shoulder now: a figure in the distance, slumped on the ground, half hidden under some kind of makeshift canopy.

Mahlia followed his gaze. 'Heloísa!'

She sped ahead of him, trudging through the thick, knee-high drifts to reach her. They both dropped down at her side beneath the waterproof sheet. It was propped up with branches, barely functional against the wind and snow. Gunnar took in her face, pale and waxen, as Mahlia pulled a bottle from the bag.

'Heloísa, can you hear us?'

The blonde woman's eyes were closed tightly against the cold. Gunnar feared the worst as he radioed Erik and told him where to drive. But then, with a groan, her eyelids fluttered open.

Thank you, God.

They propped her up against them under a blanket and she mumbled incoherently. Mahlia urged her to sip some warm water from her canteen.

'Erik's on the way,' he told Mahlia, leaning in closer, registering the woman's shortness of breath, the redness in and around her eyes. This wasn't hypothermia. This was something he recognised.

'What is it?' Mahlia demanded, her voice low.

'Check her blood pressure,' he said, as Erik's voice sounded out again on the radio.

The snowbanks they'd climbed across were pretty high, but they'd do their best to get the vehicle through. Heloísa's pulse was weak and erratic, her blood pressure dangerously low.

'I think it could be her kidneys,' he said, dread seeping deeper into his pores.

'How do you know?' Mahlia took off her coat

and wrapped it tightly around the woman's shoulders, holding her against herself.

'Experience,' he said, immediately shrugging his own jacket off and wrapping it around Mahlia. She almost refused it, but then clearly thought better of it, wrapping half of it around their survivor while he checked Heloísa. Both her legs and ankles were puffy and swollen—a sure sign that he was right.

'Oh…' Mahlia said, pursing her lips again. 'Sometimes I forget what you actually do for a living when you're not doing this.'

The wind howled like a pack of wolves as he radioed Erik again, shaking the canvas shelter with such force he thought it might rip apart. Sliding one arm around Heloísa and the other around Mahlia, he turned his back to the opening, taking the full brunt of the wind, praying Erik wasn't getting the wheels stuck in the drifts.

Mahlia leaned further into him, soothing Heloísa, who was conscious but fading fast. 'Help is coming…stay with us,' she told her. 'Your husband is fine. He's on his way to the hospital already.' Mahlia offered her more warm water, monitoring her pulse, doing her best to keep her calm.

Gunnar breathed in her damp, snowy hair and all the words he wished he could say to her built up like an army in his head while the radio stayed eerily quiet. So she was calling it off, declaring it all a mistake. He should fight for her, tell her this past week had meant more than anything had meant to him in a long, long time… And maybe he would, if he didn't keep remembering the look that had swept over her face when she'd told him she'd do anything to start a family.

Mahlia was the kind of woman he hadn't even known he needed. But he couldn't give her what *she* needed or wanted. Definitely *not* kids.

'Gunnar!'

He swung around at Erik's voice. The SAR truck's tyres were crunching on the gravel, spinning in the snow. Another vehicle had sped Rodrigo to safety, and they'd come back for them. But they didn't have long before they risked getting stuck again.

He stood, telling Mahlia to stay sheltered. Already her lips were as pale as Elioze's.

'Did you call for the chopper? Could you reach Sven?' Erik shouted.

'We might not have enough time to drive her out,' Mahlia called. 'Gunnar thinks it could be acute kidney failure. I have to say he could be right.'

'We need to get her to the hospital fast,' Gunnar confirmed, meeting her eyes. All the anger he'd seen there earlier had dissipated. They were a team. For now. 'Over land won't be fast enough.'

'Sven's on his way,' Erik told them.

Sure enough, in less than two minutes the powerful beat of the rotors filled the air, deafening them, and then the winch was being lowered precariously from the hovering chopper. With a drumming heart he worked with Mahlia and Erik to attach first Heloísa, then himself and Mahlia, so they could leave their remote perch and be lifted up into the safety of the chopper.

The snow and wind had eased enough for them to fly. Hopefully they'd done enough to get Heloísa to the medical care she needed, he thought, helping Mahlia attach a drip.

But knowing things were over with her as fast as they'd started was still hitting him repeatedly, like a ton of bricks to his brain. It didn't feel right. But what could he do? It was just the way it had to be.

Gunnar felt as if he had his heart in his throat the whole way to Reykjavik.

CHAPTER TEN

'YOU'RE GOING TO be fine, Heloísa,' Mahlia said, touching a hand to the woman's arm around the tubes.

Heloísa smiled warmly. She looked exhausted, but her cheeks had more colour in them than they'd had a couple of hours ago, when they'd rushed her through the hospital doors. The intensive care unit was busier than she'd ever seen it, but the staff had wasted no time with tests and dialysis and now she was resting in a private room.

'I'm so grateful that you and Dr Johansson found me. One of the nurses said he's famous? She said that most people get the man all wrong. What did she mean?'

Mahlia bit down on her lip. Of course a tourist from Portugal probably knew nothing about Gunnar's past. And he would like it to stay that way, she thought.

They weren't exactly in a great place, the two of them, seeing as she'd pushed him so far away from her. she might as well have shoved him off a cliff without a harness. But her heart still beat wildly, just at seeing him through the glass. He was waiting for her outside, talking on the phone.

'His family's a little messed up, that's all. It has nothing to do with him.'

'Are you...you know...together?' Heloísa asked curiously.

It was all she could do to stop her chin wobbling as she shook her head, but Heloísa had closed her eyes anyway, exhaustion taking over.

Mahlia left her to rest and closed the door softly behind her.

'I think if you hadn't seen the signs that something was wrong with her kidneys it would have been a different story,' she said, noting the telltale crease between Gunnar's eyebrows.

He shoved his phone back in his pocket quickly as she approached. She wouldn't even ask what was up, she decided. It would only annoy her more when he refused to tell her, and his secrecy wasn't her problem any more.

'Gisli,' he said quietly, motioning her to follow him down the corridor.

'Sorry?'

'That was him—messaging about tonight.'

Mahlia cursed under her breath. She'd clean forgotten they'd agreed to go for dinner at Gisli and Leo's place. The sweet couple wanted to thank them both for rescuing Leo and Katla, and they'd agreed on tonight when she'd still been deep in her infatuation bubble. They'd messaged them together, from Gunnar's bed—somewhere she would never be again, she reminded herself as tingles of desire sprang up on her skin regardless.

She already felt bad for accusing him of trying to control her. She'd panicked under his scrutiny, embarrassed that he'd called her out on the whole Javid thing. Gunnar was right: she *was* too much of a coward to face her ex, in case he doled out more emotional blackmail and made her hate herself all over again for giving in and allowing him more time with the divorce papers.

But there were so many reasons why freedom, time and having a clear mind were better for her right now than being Gunnar's secret fling. So many reasons why she'd ended it. It was just difficult to remember them all when she was next to him, and he was being so… *Gunnar.*

'I can always cancel,' he offered, holding the door open.

She stepped outside ahead of him. The sky was clear, littered with stars now. Sighing, she crossed her arms around herself and turned to him, wishing she wasn't so magnetically drawn to him that it was an act of physical restraint between her mind and her limbs not to reach for him and tell him she'd changed her mind.

'Maybe that would be best,' she forced herself to say.

Her heart fluttered in her chest as she looked up at him, thinking how her conflicting interests were probably written all over her face.

'It *would* be best,' he agreed, his steel-blue eyes holding hers like anchors. 'But Gisli said they've got the huskies out now. The sled will be waiting for us in an hour.'

Mahlia felt her eyes grow wide. For a second she couldn't speak.

Huskies?

'Doctors! I'm so happy you could make it!' Gisli, in his puffy blue ski jacket, was a ball of warm, welcoming energy as they exited Gunnar's car in the gravel car park. He lunged at them with hugs and air kisses before ushering them beyond the gate to the edge of a nature trail.

Mahlia couldn't help but gasp and laugh in awe.

Eight wide-eyed huskies barked and pawed at the snow with enthusiasm as they approached the red-and-blue-painted wooden sled. The seats were draped with sheepskin blankets that almost swallowed her in their soft white fluffiness as she sat down, taking another from Gisli to put over her lap.

'It's big enough to share,' he said, and grinned as Gunnar was made to squish in close beside her.

Before she could argue he'd tucked the blanket around them both and handed them a hip flask of moonshine each. She tucked hers away as soon as he wasn't looking. It wouldn't do to be rude, but she was *not* drinking that stuff.

'We could have taken the car, but this is more fun, no?' He winked at them, taking a seat at the front. He told them to enjoy the ride. It would be at least an hour and a half.

In seconds, they were speeding away down the small winding road and up the trail into the mountains. Mahlia couldn't help the silly grin that spread across her face as the sled jostled and shook and the pine trees whipped by in a blur of green against the snowy banks. The night sky above was an inky black canvas, lit up with stars, giving just enough light for Gisli and the dogs to navigate the way. Her heart was racing in excitement; she had never done *anything* like this.

'Gisli and Leo run a husky sled retreat,' Gunnar explained in her ear, sending tingles straight through her veins.

She realised he'd been staring at her, probably thinking she was grinning like an idiot.

'Usually this is reserved for tourists.'

'Well, I guess I am a tourist,' she said, tucking her hair back self-consciously just as the sled flew over a rock and almost sent them flying.

Her hand flew to Gunnar's knee impulsively and he pressed a firm hand over hers, under the blanket. Before she could even think, she was holding his hand. Neither of them let go.

The dogs wound expertly across frozen lakes and rivers, past chunky-legged Icelandic horses and through snow-covered pine forests. She pretended to sip from her flask in silence, until Gisli stopped the dogs in the middle of an open meadow. She didn't have to ask why. The northern lights were dancing joyously above them in greens, pinks and purples, as if an artist had spilt an entire paint box across the sky. The only sound was the dogs' panting and the whoosh of wind in the branches as they watched the impossible beauty of this moving picture amongst the stars.

Amazing!

When she turned to Gunnar in awe, sucking in the icy, crisp air, perfumed with pine, the aurora shone back at her from his eyes. It sent a flood of something so pure and magical through her bloodstream she almost felt as if she was floating. This moment was perfection.

'You know, apart from when I saw you playing that guitar, I don't think you've ever looked as radiant as you do now,' he told her, his grip on her hand tightening.

His voice was anguished, and full of longing, and Mahlia held her breath, feeling her stomach twist into knots as she watched the emotions play across his face. He wanted to kiss her. And she wanted nothing more than to kiss him, too. Every fibre of her body was telling her to make the move as desire coiled deep inside her, but no... Logic *must* prevail. If she acted on her impulses now, when would she stop?

'Stop...' she whispered, closing her eyes and letting go of his hand. 'I told you...'

'I know, I know,' he growled from somewhere deep in his throat.

And her heart thrummed in pain as she felt him ball his fist at his side against her thigh.

The dinner plates were already on the table when Leo welcomed them all inside to the warmth. She was pleased to see he was walking just fine after his accident.

Every inch of the cosy lodge seemed to have been delicately crafted in a classic Swedish style, from the exposed logs on the walls to the plush sheepskin rugs. In one corner an enormous fireplace roared, its heat inviting Mahlia closer as she looked around—everywhere but at Gunnar.

That almost-kiss in the sled was still playing on her mind, but she hadn't caved. She could be proud of herself for that, at least.

Katla padded up to give them a good sniff, wagging her tail, and Gunnar got down on his haunches to pet her. Damn him for looking so handsome and sexy stroking a dog...was there anything that *didn't* make him look good?

Mahlia gave him a wide berth as she walked around him to where Leo was stirring something in a cast iron cauldron on the open fire. 'It smells so good,' she told him, taking a lungful of the delicious aroma.

'Reindeer stew, like Gisli promised.' He smiled. 'We always cook it like this for our guests. Take a seat!'

Mahlia's phone pinged just as she was about to sit at the table. She didn't miss Gunnar's eyes on her as she pulled it out. He probably thought it was Javid, and so did she for a moment.

'It's Inka,' she announced, scanning the message. 'The rest of the prototypes have arrived. She's just signed for them, before she goes out to meet Demus in Reykjavik.'

'Demus?' Gunnar cocked an eyebrow.

Mahlia couldn't help smiling as he peered over her shoulder at the message. 'I think she's trying to tell us she's going on a date with your brother. You know, I could tell they had chemistry the other day! I think that's so great—good for them.'

Gunnar just nodded thoughtfully. She could see he was stewing more than the reindeer. 'He kept that one a secret,' he said after a moment, scratching his chin and pulling out his phone as if a confirmation from Demus might pop up, telling him about his date.

'He's not the only one who's good at keeping secrets,' she quipped, before she could stop herself.

He scowled darkly as he took a seat opposite her at the table. Thankfully any planned retort was shut down as Leo and Gisli placed steaming bowls of stew in front of them and launched into a conversation about the nice Australian tourists who'd left them some biscuits called Tim Tams after their five-star husky sledding holiday with them.

She liked this couple a lot, thought Mahlia as they ate and talked, and the dogs barked occasionally outside. If they were picking up on any tension between her and Gunnar they weren't saying so.

But she'd have to talk to him eventually, she thought, feeling hot at the idea. They hadn't exactly had closure…

Sometime later, over a dessert of hot apple strudel, which Mahlia had to admit was just as good as the reindeer stew, Gisli asked if she'd consider sending some of her prototypes to them, for their guests. She'd told them about the venture over dinner, and he'd said he'd heard about it. Everyone knew everyone here, after all.

'We need to test them properly first,' she told him. 'But you can look at some when we're certain the design is ready.'

'I think some of our less mobile guests would enjoy that,' he said thoughtfully. 'They like riding the sled, so why not taking the trails independently too? It would open up a lot more opportunities for us and them. You know, it's great to see your brother getting involved, too, Dr Johansson. He's really quite the ambassador already.'

Mahlia felt her breath catch as Gunnar put his fork down. She hadn't mentioned Demus at all. Then Gisli pulled his phone out, showing them the team photo that had been taken for the website that day. It had somehow made it onto social media anyway—one of the other participants on the trial must have reposted it.

She waited nervously for Gunnar's reaction, but he met her eyes as if grounding himself and sat back in his seat, drumming his fingers on the table. Maybe he was starting to realise it wasn't such a big deal, she thought hopefully. The Johanssons were out and about, living their 'normal' lives just like everyone else. The world hadn't ended, had it?

Eventually, Gisli got to his feet. She thought he was going to offer to drive them back, and went to find her jacket, yawning behind her hand.

But he said, 'Are you guys ready to see your room?'

Mahlia's stomach dropped. Gunnar looked at her in surprise. They were expected to stay over? She was totally unprepared for this, but they were so far off the grid at this tourist resort she probably should have expected it.

'Everything you might need is in there. And on a night like this,' Gisli continued, leading them to the door, 'I think you'll *really* appreciate the ceiling.'

CHAPTER ELEVEN

BEHIND THE LODGE, in the centre of the camp, connected by a series of wooden walkways that criss-crossed the premises like a lattice, were a series of stunning, sleek, modern tepees that took Mahlia's breath away. Each one seemed to be equipped with its own layer of glass panels on top, held firmly in place by steel frames and bolted to the ground.

Gisli unzipped one, beckoning them inside, and she pressed a hand to her mouth in shock. The glass ceiling acted as a viewing panel above them, perfect for stargazers and for watching the northern lights from the bed. The huge, comfy-looking king-sized bed was complete with even more sheepskin blankets. A small wood-burning fire was already blazing behind a glass door.

'This is incredible!' Mahlia exclaimed.

Gunnar looked embarrassed, at best.

'The others are already booked, for guests

who'll arrive early tomorrow, but I figured you wouldn't mind sharing this one.'

Gisli winked at her and she felt her cheeks flame. So the couple had clearly picked up on *something* between them, despite their recent rift. Was it that obvious?

'This will be fine. More than fine—thank you,' she said quickly, dropping to the bed.

Gisli bade them goodnight and zipped up the canvas door behind him. The silence was overwhelming, but the northern lights had come out to play again. She'd focus on that, she thought, while Gunnar slept on the... On the what? There was no couch here—just the rugs on the floor.

'Sorry about this. I didn't even think...' he started, walking around the bed, inspecting the wooden dresser, the ornate lamp, the tiny attached bathroom.

'It's not your fault,' she said, taking off her shoes, watching the way his muscled frame cast long, slender shadows across the bed in the firelight. 'This *is* incredible. Look at the lights. I could get never get tired of those monsters coming at me.'

Gunnar huffed a small laugh, shrugged off his boots and climbed onto the bed beside her, thumping an overly soft pillow into shape before putting his head on it. Her heart went wild at his proximity, but she kept to her side, her pillow, and focused her eyes on the blackness of the sky, studded with stars and decorated with dancing green swirls.

'I'm not like him, you know,' Gunnar said suddenly, through the silence. 'Your ex. I would *never* try and control you…not intentionally.'

'I know. I'm sorry I said that to you earlier,' she said, and sighed.

He sniffed, fixing his own eyes on the ceiling. 'And as for my secrets… I didn't want you getting involved in what's going on with my mother, but I shouldn't have shut you out completely. That wasn't fair.'

Her body tensed. She continued to watch the lights move through the glass roof. They weren't a couple any more—if they ever had been to begin with. She should just accept his apology and move on, take this as closure. But she wanted to know what was causing this pain to radiate from his every pore. So she asked him what was going on *really*.

His voice was so sorrowful as he answered that she found her eyes straining against tears, and her chest felt so tight she thought she might burst. Finally, as if unplugging a valve that had been bursting to be free, Gunnar told her exactly how lost and sick his mother really was—mind, body and soul. How he and Demus had tried to get her help for years, but she'd kept on refusing, waiting for her husband to come back for her. He told her how it had torn him up, wanting to protect her but only creating more problems for himself and Demus as he did so—as if that was *his* fault.

She told him that it wasn't, and confided in him about her own struggles. How her mother's depression had spiralled several years ago, after her sister had died—Mahlia's auntie Jazz—and how not even her father had been able to bring her out of it. They'd started recommending that Mahlia not visit them on weekends like she'd used to, which had only pushed her even further into the grip of Javid's toxic control.

Then Gunnar opened up about the reporters who liked to follow them and hang around his mother's house, waiting for something juicy to boost their click rates.

'I didn't want this to end up with everyone talking about *you*,' he said. 'I don't think I could handle someone else just…'

'Leaving you because of your family? I know.'

She reached for his hand despite herself, feeling closer to him than ever after what he'd just confided. As if she'd ever leave him because of anything someone else had done.

But it was more than that with her—it was the fear of someone leaving her, if she ever decided to trust a man enough to let one in again. The fear of losing herself.

'Look, Demus is fine, isn't he?' she continued. 'No one thinks anything's wrong with him being involved with the bikes or Inka. And I'm not like your ex, either. You are the man I...' She tailed off, surprised and slightly embarrassed by what she'd been about to say. 'You've come to be really important to me.'

Composing herself, she sat up, hugging her knees.

'Gunnar, it's just... I came here to be *me* for once. Not to—'

'I know. And I don't want to stand in your way.'

She let out a long sigh that turned into a groan, pressing her palms to her eyes. 'The funny thing is, I've never felt more *me* than I do in the moments when I'm with you. And that's a little scary. I have a whole bunch of what-ifs going round in my head. What if Javid doesn't let me go...?'

He sat up, matching her stance, arms around his knees. 'You're in control of that outcome, Mahlia. Only you.'

She swallowed tightly, wanting to be honest. 'But there's more...about you...going round and round and round. *What if he likes me? What if he doesn't? What if I fall in love and then...?*'

'What if he doesn't want kids?' Gunnar finished, making her turn to him.

'Kids?'

'You said you wanted them someday. I don't, by the way. I don't want any children—ever.'

Mahlia swallowed, wishing her heart hadn't just raced like a freight train to her frontal lobe, screeching a warning at her. 'You don't?' she managed, trying to hide her disappointment.

'It wouldn't be fair...' He sighed. 'All things considered.'

All things considered?

She frowned at him. 'Because you're ashamed of your name, you mean? Your name is something any child should grow up to be proud of, Gunnar.'

'Maybe *you* think so,' he muttered.

'A lot of people think so. Why else would we be here? Look at where we are now because of you. You help people, Gunnar. I don't think I've met anyone more impressive, actually. Well, maybe your brother. He's pretty cool...'

He cut her off with a soft groan. His warm hand swept across the curve of her face, cupping her chin gently before he pressed his lips to hers, testing her.

Mahlia looped her arms around him. Resistance to his kisses was futile. She knew she should resist... She needed things in the future that he couldn't give her…unless…unless just having him, and *this*, was enough?

It felt like enough right now.

Laying her down again gently against the sheepskin, Gunnar traced his hands along her body, exploring the contours of her neck and shoulders, kissing her with a concentrated intensity and a connection to her soul that threw all their previous encounters into shadow.

'I'll stop if you want me to,' he said, hovering over her on his forearms.

And the hunger in his eyes told her how hard he would find that. As hard as she would.

The aurora played above them, giving him an emerald halo, and she knew it was pointless even trying to deny herself or him—even if this wasn't something that could ever last.

'No, don't stop,' she whispered, and pulled him back to her lips.

She surrendered completely into a passionate kiss, shuddering as his fingertips ran lightly over her collarbone, before travelling softly down the line of her spine, feeling their way across every vertebra, making her skin prickle in pleasure.

How did he do this to her?

Tingles took over her flesh as he caressed her curves, and when he moved even lower, lingering over the swell of her hips and the smooth planes of her thighs, she arched into him with a ragged sigh, opening herself further to him. Whatever he wanted to do, she'd reciprocate. She was undeniably his in this moment...beyond the point of no return. His lips trailed blissfully behind his fingertips as they travelled, exploring every inch of her body as she trembled.

'Gunnar...' she moaned, wiping at her eyes, clutching fistfuls of his hair.

So this was what it was like to be completely overwhelmed by a million sensations... The heat of their desire grew like a wildfire, consuming them both in its intensity until they were making love—real love, she realised, as they moved as one in a hot jumble of blankets. This was like nothing else she had ever experienced. In this moment, nothing else mattered but them.

When the night had passed in a blur of lovemaking, and the faint morning sun was peering through the glass roof, Mahlia awoke to find Gunnar gone. A faint shuffling sound outside had her pulling on a robe and opening the canvas door.

'Good morning.'

She blinked as Gunnar held out a hand, and she stepped from the tepee, hardly believing her eyes. Pancakes, poached eggs and bacon, freshly baked pastries and a pot of tea with honey were waiting on a little terrace table under a giant heat lamp. He pulled out a chair for her, poured her tea, and she marvelled at how good he looked, considering they'd barely slept.

The mountains glistened with snow beyond the pine trees as they ate, touching feet under the table, and the sound of the dogs fussing around the guesthouse was strangely calming.

'Gisli will drive us back when we're ready,' he said.

'I don't want to go back. Can we just stay here for ever?' she pleaded, noticing how the napkins were embroidered with little husky dogs. She felt as if she was in a dream. 'Last night was amazing...'

'Thank you for listening,' he said, taking her hand across the table. 'I haven't spoken to anyone like that for—well, *ever*.'

'Your mother's going to be OK,' she told him, swallowing back a flock of butterflies. 'So is Demus, and so are you.'

'I hope you're right,' he said, running a thumb across her knuckles. 'I made the call this morning. We're taking her to the Five Lakes Rehabilitation Centre on Saturday. Whether she wants to go or not.'

Mahlia told him that she'd be there; she'd go with him if he wanted. He didn't reply, which set her on edge a moment, before she realised he'd opened up more to her than he ever had before last night, and that was a pretty big deal for him—especially as she was still married, not available, and wholly unsuitable, really, if he didn't want children...

Oh, my God, stop, Mahlia! Just be happy for him!

She had helped him realise he didn't have to go through everything alone—that he could involve people in his life without fearing they'd run a mile if things got shaky.

Maybe he'd meet someone else after she'd gone home to New Zealand, she thought suddenly, as he talked about the rehabilitation centre's facilities and poured her more tea. He would meet someone who belonged here, not halfway across the world. Someone who didn't want to bring children into a relationship.

Ugh. Why were her stupid thoughts ruining the moment again? Could she not just enjoy this little fantasy of being treated well and appreciated while it lasted?

Gunnar stood and pulled her to her feet, kissing her softly, but with so much heart she wanted to drag him right back to bed. In fact she might have done so, if her phone hadn't started to ring with the dreaded ringtone she'd reserved for Javid.

She pulled away gently, resting her head on his shoulder with a sigh.

'That's him, isn't it?' Gunnar said into her neck, and she nodded.

He took her shoulders now, making her look at him. 'Answer it,' he said.

She sucked in a breath, searching his blue eyes. 'And say what? That I spent the night in a tepee at a husky retreat, having crazy sex with my winchman under the northern lights?'

'Sure—why not? And put him on speakerphone.'

She snorted with horror. 'Gunnar! No!'

Frustration glimmered in his eyes. 'The longer you don't answer, the longer you're going to torture yourself, wondering what he wants.'

'I know what he wants. He wants to remind me how good we were together. How there's no one for me except him.'

'So tell him he's wrong.'

'I will. I just...'

He stepped back from her, starting to gather up the cups and plates, and she cursed herself under her breath. He was biting back his words in case she accused him of trying to control her actions again. They'd just gone round in a circle... Stupid. *Stupid.*

Ramming her hands through her hair, she reached for her phone, let her finger hover over the answer button. She should just pick up. Gunnar was right—this was insane!

Pick up, Mahlia! Tell Javid you've had enough. Tell him if he doesn't sign the papers by the end of the day, you'll have a court summons on his doorstep by next week.

That was what she should do. That was what she'd imagined saying to him so many times. Yet her finger still wouldn't swipe. Just seeing his name sent waves of dread so intense through her body she needed to sit down. If she answered, he'd steal back the power she'd regained. He'd make everything she'd done here, away from him, smaller, less important. He'd make it all about him and leave her feeling worse, like he always did.

No one understood what it was like, living every moment in fear of losing yourself, having your autonomy pulled out from underneath you and stomped on. It wasn't something you could just wish away and make disappear. Seven years... Seven years had a lasting effect—like a ripple through everything she did. And now she was an incorrigible coward on top.

But it was almost as if Javid knew...as if he'd *sensed* what she was doing and was hellbent on ruining her high. She could almost picture him storming into the tepee, berating her, telling her she looked ridiculous, that no man would put up with her for long, that she'd do better just coming home to him. Either that or he'd cry again. Beg again.

The phone rang and rang until she flicked it onto silent mode. Still, it rang.

Coward, the voice in her head accused, when eventually he gave up.

Turning around with a sigh of relief, she realised Gunnar was standing in the doorway, watching her.

'We should go,' he said gruffly, grabbing up his jacket.

CHAPTER TWELVE

GUNNAR WATCHED DEMUS take another corner on the trail up ahead, the sunshine blazing off the pristine e-bike as he and three more trial participants zoomed at full speed. The snow was finally clearing, with fewer storms per day, so for the last few days, with only one SAR call-out to deal with, they'd been here every afternoon, and Mahlia was in her element.

Everyone wanted a piece of her and her ideas, it seemed. From the press to the Wilderness Association, to the CEO of the Icelandic Disability Alliance. Gunnar had kept his distance from the cameras. But with her, for the first time in his life, he wasn't the first person people looked at when they walked into a room.

'Demus looks so happy,' Mahlia said now, as Inka steered up to their side, grinning broadly. 'And I'm sure you have something to do with that smile on his face,' she teased her friend.

Inka grinned behind her blonde hair. He noticed the way both women shot him a querying look, but he pretended not to see. The jury was still out on what to make of this blossoming relationship, and he was trying not to let his fierce protection of Demus cloud his views. Maybe he was also a little jealous...

'These prototypes are incredible, Mahlia,' Inka said. 'We had another company asking when they can buy them this morning.'

'I need to work on securing a manufacturer in Europe,' Mahlia told her thoughtfully, and Gunnar listened as they discussed the bikes, his eyes never leaving his brother.

Demus did look happy. Deliriously happy. To be riding the bike, to be in control, to be dating a great woman who understood his struggles. He deserved it, Gunnar thought. He couldn't picture himself like that—being comfortable, carefree, happy, without the gnawing feeling that it was all about to fall apart for one reason or another. These calls from Mahlia's ex weren't helping...

Still, despite his head and his heart telling him it was a bad idea to take this further, to involve her in his life, she'd wriggled into his heart enough for him to break down a few walls in front of her. Enough for her to forget she'd tried to end things and now had offered to come with him and Demus to his mother's house this afternoon. Enough for him to go along with it all.

He'd almost refused to let her come, point-blank, several times, but it *had* felt good opening up to someone…to feel that maybe he didn't have to do everything alone.

Even if she wanted a life he couldn't give her.

Even if she was still bound to her ex, and on the verge of going back to New Zealand.

Even if she might realise at any minute that being caught on camera with him in any precarious situation would get her a very different kind of publicity from that surrounding these e-bikes.

Who was he to deny her something she wanted to do for him? She'd been repressed enough, and he was not about to come off as a control freak.

'Are you worried about this afternoon?' Mahlia whispered now, touching his shoulder.

She must have seen the look on his face. Instinctively he whipped his head around to look for cameras, but all the photographers had taken their shots of the bikes already and were long gone. He willed himself to relax…not to step away from her.

'A little,' he confessed, surprising himself by admitting his emotions.

Ma didn't know yet, but they were about to ruin her day. The Five Lakes Rehabilitation Centre was expecting them.

Pulling up around the corner from the house, Gunnar found his hands gripping the steering wheel till his knuckles were white.

'Where are they?' Demus asked from the back seat, checking his phone. 'They were meant to...'

'I think this is them,' Mahlia said, one hand on the door.

Sure enough, a van was pulling up behind them—away from the house, as he'd instructed, so Ma couldn't anticipate their arrival and try to run away.

Two male staff members from Five Lakes exited the vehicle in their off-white uniforms and jackets and, to his surprise, Mahlia got out to meet them with him, helping him get Demus's wheelchair unloaded in record time.

Just having her here, he realised, was giving him strength and courage. Not that he was calm—not by a long shot! His heart was pounding a million miles an hour as they followed the staff up the driveway and rang the bell. Next door, the curtains twitched, and Demus waved at their elderly female neighbour. Mrs Sigurðsson loathed them all. Mahlia too offered a wave, at which the old woman scowled and drew the curtains across roughly.

'Who is it?' came his mother's voice from behind the shiny black door.

Gunnar swallowed the golf ball in his throat, glancing behind them for any lurking opportunist photographers.

'Mrs Johansson, we're here to help you,' one

of the staff said in Icelandic as the door opened slowly.

Ma peered out, her red, bloated face and bloodshot eyes telling them all she'd been on the bottle today already—probably since the minute she'd woken up.

There was a crash of glass shattering on the floor before Ma tried to slam the door shut again, crying, *'No!'*

Demus wheeled his chair into the doorway, forcing it to stay open.

'Ma, you have to go with them,' Gunnar said kindly but firmly, his boots crunching on the broken glass as Mahlia stepped inside with him.

Ma stumbled up the stairs, unsteady on her feet, 'I should… I should pack then.' He and Mahlia ran after her, would she really pack, or would she try to escape through a window?. 'I'll pack an overnight bag,' she slurred, and his heart ached as it became clear his mother was deeply uncomfortable, even in her intoxication, and obviously in denial.

Mahlia was strong. 'It's going to be OK,' she said gently to his mother.

'Well, where are we going, exactly?'

'Trust us, Ma,' he soothed, struggling not to let his voice crack.

'Well, how long will I be gone for? I can't be gone too long, you know that.'

Gunnar told her where she was going, and said they weren't sure how long for yet. 'It's for your own good, Ma. I'm sorry. It's the best thing to do to keep you safe.'

'Everyone just wants you to get better,' Mahlia said now.

Gunnar knew she didn't need to know Icelandic to see that his mother was stuttering every excuse she could think of now, as to why she didn't need to go for longer than one night.

'And who are *you*?' Ma asked, pulling up short in front of Mahlia.

'She's with Gunnar, Ma. Don't make a scene, please,' Demus said coolly.

The Five Lakes staff soon had her out through the door, explaining gently and calmly again where they were taking her, saying that everything was arranged.

'I packed her a bag a few days ago,' Demus told them. 'I had my carer leave it on top of the wardrobe in her bedroom.'

'I'll get it.' Mahlia was already hurrying up the stairs.

Dread pooled in Gunnar's stomach as he followed after her.

Oh, God, no. He could only imagine the state of it up there…

'Which one is her room?' she asked, stopping on the landing. The open doorway to the left and the revealing stench of stale alcohol sent her forward. She stepped over a pile of clothes and stopped short in the dank, dark room, pressing a hand to her mouth at the sight.

The room was a mess, the bed unmade, the walls streaked with spilt red wine and candle wax. Clothes, empty bottles and takeaway containers were strewn haphazardly across the floor. The musty smell of years of alcohol consumption lingered in the air, as if it had soaked into the very fabric of the house he and Demus had used to play in. This place held so many happy memories, but now, in this sad, sorrowful room, every single one of them felt like a lie.

Mahlia took a few steps further in, and he saw her mouth turning down in dismay as she took in the curtains, drawn tight over sash windows that hadn't been opened in months. A small bedside table was cluttered with bottles and glasses, and the ashtray overflowing on top of it made him wince. Ma clearly smoked in bed every day. It was worse than he'd thought. She'd done her best to hide the extent of her troubles when she'd known people were coming, but alone, she was… broken.

A wooden wardrobe stood in one corner, its doors wide open, revealing more discarded clothes inside. Mahlia reached up high, locating Ma's bag.

'Is this it?'

She turned to him with it. Then, taking one look at his face, she dropped it immediately and crossed to him, wrapping her arms tight around his middle.

Gunnar realised he'd been watching her taking it all in through clouded eyes, his fists clenched in his hair as he stood in the doorway. Only now, in her arms, did he blink the tears free. Shame and embarrassment burned his cheeks as he wiped them away quickly. He itched to pull away from her, to create as much distance as possible before she did it first—because surely she would leave him after this? How could she not? But at the same time he never wanted her to let go.

She held him till Demus called out from downstairs. 'Did you guys find it?'

'Coming!' Mahlia called back. 'This must be so hard for you,' she whispered, caressing his cheek. Her face was contorted in sympathy. 'Are you OK?'

'I'm just sorry you have to see this,' he croaked, picking up the bag with shaking hands.

He couldn't even look her in the eye right now. Instead he muttered another apology for having exposed her to this, the full extent of the chaos-tinged mess that was his reality, and thought that this was yet another reminder of why bringing children into his world would be a very bad idea.

* * *

They followed the van under an ever-darkening sky, and behind the wheel Gunnar tried not to imagine how terrified Ma must be, strapped in there with the staff.

'She's going to be fine…you've done the right thing,' Mahlia assured him softly.

He glanced over at her in the passenger seat. She'd been so understanding and supportive throughout this whole ordeal. She'd never know what that meant to him. But *was* he doing the right thing with Ma? With her?

His chest felt like a lead weight.

She seemed to sense his consternation and gave his hand a reassuring squeeze. Gunnar took a deep breath, steeling himself for the rehab clinic: the doctors, nurses and social workers who would all swarm around Ma soon enough. They'd figure out the best way to help her get better—he had to believe that. But what if it was too late? What if none of them—none of this— was able to make a difference?

A motorbike appeared ahead, its headlights swerving erratically. Mahlia gasped and gripped the door. 'He has a camera!'

She whipped her head around as the bike fell in behind them, then sped up again. There were two people on it: a rider in leathers, wearing a black helmet, his face obscured by its tinted visor, and a smaller figure on the back in a full-face cover, holding a huge camera.

Gunnar's heart sank as he hit the gas harder, clenched the wheel tighter.

'They know where this road goes,' Demus said from the back. 'They must have followed us from Reykjavik. How did they even know...?'

'Everyone will know now. Cover your face,' Gunnar told Mahlia, his eyes on the road.

His heart was racing...his tongue felt thick. There was nowhere to pull over and the motor-bike kept pace, weaving between them and the van. Whoever was behind the camera kept snap-ping, even when Mahlia—who hadn't covered her face at all—rolled the window down and yelled at them.

'Get out of here! This is none of your busi-ness!'

Demus chuckled into his hands, like he always did when he was overwhelmed by drama.

Gunnar closed the window on her, trying to keep his seething anger in check. 'Ignore them,' he instructed, feeling his jaw harden as she glow-ered through the windshield at the bike.

He was hopeful they'd be gone for good by the time Mahlia helped him escort Ma up the snow-lined steps to the grey, mansion-like fa-cility of the rehabilitation centre, which fringed the National Park. But just as they reached the veranda he saw it: the glimmer of a lens peeking from the trees at the perimeter, just beyond the security wall.

No sooner had he swung around to confront whoever was there than the branches rustled and the stealth photographer disappeared. In seconds the roar of the motorbike's engine told him they were getting away.

Ma was still making a scene in his arms. There was nothing Gunnar could do but let them go.

CHAPTER THIRTEEN

Mahlia curled her legs up on the couch, watching Gunnar's fingers flying over the piano keys. The snow swirled in tiny flakes outside—nothing like the blizzards she had grown accustomed to. She could read him well by now, and could tell when he was bottling things up. Right now he was taking his frustration over those photos out on the poor piano, with a million thoughts creasing his brow, and she knew he felt guilty over the press furore.

They'd been here three nights already. Gunnar had suggested it, of course. No one knew where the cabin was, as opposed to their homes in Reykjavik, and when Demus had last called he'd said there were still photographers and camera crews outside their apartments, as well as at the gates of Five Lakes.

It was a bigger deal than she'd anticipated, admittedly, the fact that the once-loved TV news anchor and renowned alcoholic Kaðlín Johansson was finally being admitted to rehab. And she understood now why Gunnar had been so wary of the media all this time—how they could pull the rug out from under someone before they could even blink.

'Get the guitar,' Gunnar said to her now, swivelling on the piano stool, but Mahlia shook her head.

'I don't want to play,' she told him, failing to keep the frustration from her voice.

Javid was calling off the hook again in her pocket—so much so that she'd almost answered earlier. She was ready now, she realised. She'd been ready to have it out with him for days. Something about being here for Gunnar, knowing he valued her the way she'd always wanted to be valued, instead of owned and ordered around, had given her the courage to kick Javid out of her life once and for all.

But the signal here was bad. It would take three times as long to talk to him here, with the line cutting out every three seconds.

'Gunnar, we need to get back to the city.'

'You're free to go,' he said abruptly.

Of course, he would say that.

'I'll have someone fetch you and drive you back in an unmarked car.'

'I don't want to go without you,' she told him quietly.

Her mind was spinning. Part of her knew she

should go without him. Javid aside, the longer she bound herself to Gunnar, the harder it would be to tear herself away for good and go after the life she wanted—two kids and all, however she might have to get them! But then again… She couldn't imagine a future without Gunnar in it any more. Maybe it wouldn't be so bad…just the two of them. It wasn't as if she didn't have enough to keep her busy!

'I shouldn't have put you in this situation,' he said, clutching her waist, making those butterflies start up again in her belly.

'I chose to come with you, and…' She sighed into the top of his head. He was wearing the sweater she'd kept up till now. 'Gunnar, all that matters is that your mother receives the help she needs to get better.'

Her words fell on deaf ears. 'As soon as you get back there will be someone waiting for you, Mahlia. They'll all want a piece of you now.'

'Maybe so…' She sank back to the couch again with a sigh, looking at the article about them still face-up on his iPad. The TV was on, on mute—something about a volcano making noises somewhere—but she couldn't focus on anything.

Gunnar went back to playing the piano despondently. Her phone buzzed. Javid again. He must know exactly where in Iceland she was now and who she was with, thanks to the news. Oh,

God, what if he came for her? She just had to get back now, to Reykjavik. Have that one-to-one talk with him on the phone in private...get it over with. She'd do it tonight.

'Gunnar,' she said, 'maybe you should call me that car. I'm going back to Reykjavik.'

She went and packed her bag to the sound of his piano-playing, noting when he stopped to pace the room, hearing his feet padding across the floor. The sheets were still strewn halfway down the bed, messed up from their lovemaking. Why had she kept on sleeping with him? Because their connection was so strong it was practically impossible to deny herself, and being with him like that felt like plugging into a life source.

Maybe it's enough. Him and me, together.

'Don't forget this,' Gunnar said, handing her her phone the second she stepped back into the room with her bag. 'I called for a car.'

'OK.'

She was about to thank him, and reach up for a kiss, but he walked away from her, shoulders hunched as he leaned against the kitchen counter, studying her.

Instincts primed, she slid her phone into her pocket, crossed her arms. 'Gunnar...?'

He narrowed his blue eyes at her, then looked to the floor, making her heart skid. Something was wrong.

'Gunnar, please don't worry about me going back. I'll be fine.'

'I can't keep doing this,' he said. 'And I don't know how you can either.'

Her stomach dropped. 'Doing what?'

'Mahlia, we both know this is going to end eventually. We've said it all before. It's not just about the press…' He gestured around the cabin, at the iPad and the TV. 'I can't give you what you want. I'm just casting more and more shadows over you and your future.'

Oh, God. So he was doing it. Really ending it for good. Her knees felt weak. She'd felt it coming in the silences between their conversations; in the way he'd been looking at her all day.

'But what if you're enough for me and having children doesn't matter?' she tried, suddenly panicked. Her heart was racing now and her voice felt small, choked.

'You'd only come to resent me,' he said gravely, studying her face.

Mahlia felt frozen to the spot, as if her world was getting colder by the second.

'You want kids, and we both know that *does* matter to you. But that's not what I want, Mahlia. I'm not lying to myself about that, and you shouldn't lie to yourself about what you want either.'

Rage bubbled up within her. 'Don't tell me

what to do or what I think or need.' She couldn't help it now. The tears were bristling in her eyes and her palms felt clammy.

He stepped closer, pressing a long kiss to her forehead that felt so final it broke her heart.

'I'm doing this to save you.'

'What?'

OK, that was totally not necessary.

She shoved at his chest—hard. 'I don't need you to *save* me from anything, Gunnar. I just want *you*. And if you don't trust that that's enough for me, then you're right—this should end.'

He closed his eyes, drew his lips together for a moment, and she felt her heart shatter.

'It's not that I don't trust you. I just know you, Mahlia.'

'No, you don't. Don't think you know me. If you knew me, you'd know I can make up my own damn mind about what I need in my life!'

Gunnar sank to the couch, buried his face in his hands, shaking his head. When her car pulled up he didn't get up and walk outside with her. He simply tossed a heavy log onto the fire and refused to look at her.

Gunnar woke the next morning with a headache. The bed was empty beside him, as expected. He checked his phone, seeing zero missed calls from Mahlia. As if she would have called him after what he'd done. But he'd done the right thing. He had already caused her enough trouble. He wouldn't keep stringing her along selfishly, telling himself he was enough for her.

OK, so there had been moments when he'd felt his resolve weaken—she'd been resilient enough over this whole media debacle with his mother to assure him that maybe she'd stick around if things got tough, so she wasn't another Idina. But no... His being with her was still selfish. She was kidding herself, and him, if she thought she could sacrifice having children for him!

Slinging the sheets back, he went to hit the shower, trying to drown the relentless thwack of pain to his brain whenever he thought about her—and also about what he'd seen on her overturned phone the second he'd picked it up last night.

In the living room, he flicked on the TV just as Demus called.

'Can you believe those scientists took the mayor out there?' Demus sounded worried.

'Where?' Gunnar yawned, sloshing some coffee into a chipped mug.

'To the village...the one in the news, right in the lava's path!'

'There's no lava yet. Nothing's happened,' Inka told him in the background.

So, they were together now? Something like envy rattled him.

'That volcano has been dormant for decades,' he heard her say.

'But it's rumbling, Inks. I don't trust it,' Demus said.

Gunnar slugged his coffee. He was only half listening. That text message was still burning all other thoughts from his brain.

As he'd handed her phone back to her last night, before he'd called for a car to take her back to the city, he'd had to force his brain to wrap itself around the fact that Javid was the reason she'd wanted to leave, really. Her ex's message had been right there in his hands, on her phone, along with a photo of his smug face.

He couldn't unsee it now.

Mahlia, I'm in Reykjavik. Ready when you are.

When and why the hell she'd agreed to let her ex come all the way here from New Zealand, who knew? He'd been too angry at the thought of her finally succumbing to her ex's pleas for her attention to even question her about it. She'd had every chance to admit that she was putting herself in his line of fire in person, but she hadn't said a word.

He seethed as his mind reeled.

It didn't matter now. They were over.

Don't think any more about it, or her, he told himself, grappling for any bricks he could find to put up a wall in his mind before the pain rushed back in. *She's leaving for New Zealand soon anyway. You always knew you had a time limit! She was always going to leave. You can't give her what she needs.*

'Oh, man… What the…?' Demus was still on the line. 'Gunnar?'

'If it's just a little rumble it's probably not a big deal…'

'Not the volcano. Gunnar, it's Dad.'

Gunnar flicked to the channel his brother was watching. His heart raced like a runaway train as he stared at the screen, his mind swirling. It was his father, standing outside the Five Lakes Rehabilitation Centre. The man was almost unrecognisable in sunglasses, a hat, and a thick winter coat flapping around his too-thin frame.

'I can't believe it,' Gunnar muttered, as at least seven microphones were shoved in his father's pale, drawn face.

'He looks…different…' Demus said softly, as if afraid to break the spell.

No one spoke for a few moments, listening to him address the flock of reporters who'd never stopped swarming around the front entrance to Five Lakes. They had an even juicier story now.

He'd seen his wife on the news, he said. He'd been shocked into action at the look on her face as they'd admitted her. He said his heart had been shattered, hearing her say she'd been waiting for him all this time, afraid to go anywhere too far in case he came home for her. He apologised, called himself a coward. He said he'd let himself, his country, and worst of all his family down.

Inka broke the spell in the end. 'Well?' she said in the background. 'Are you going to go and see him, or not?'

Gunnar's heart jumped into his throat.

Mahlia stared at the phone screen, watching the morning news replay in a stupor. The water she was sitting by in the shadow of the cathedral fell clean away. First the shock of Javid descending on her in Reykjavik without warning, and now this!

Simmering as she studied the man on the screen, she could hardly believe it. So *this* small, sheepish-looking, skinny man was Gunnar's once lauded and powerful father, who'd helped bring this country to its knees. Back from Cambodia, or wherever he'd been hiding.

Gunnar looked less than impressed, standing there at the Five Lakes rehab centre with him and Demus, the photographers all snapping around them like piranhas. But at least he'd gone there.

She couldn't help being impressed with him for that, despite their argument.

Should she call him? No...of course she shouldn't. He'd broken things off, even after she'd told him that being just the two of them would be enough for her!

Not that there wasn't still some niggling doubt in her mind about that. She sighed. Maybe he did know her better than she thought. Maybe he *was* right to try and 'save' her from another huge mistake, putting another man before her own needs.

At least she'd drawn enough strength from Gunnar to have it out with Javid once and for all, in person. Which was not what she'd been expecting to do at all when she'd come back to the city.

Mahlia, I'm in Reykjavik. Ready when you are.

She'd almost thrown her phone away, seeing that he'd flown here and was 'ready' for her. What the hell did that even *mean*? When the message had come in she'd been packing her bags at the cabin, so she hadn't seen it till she was already on the way to Reykjavik, but pure fury and fire—no doubt a result of Gunnar's bombshell too—had propelled her to Javid's hotel.

The universe had clearly told her to grow a

pair, to knock on his door and tell him to his face, in a way he understood, that she was sick of this, that there was no way in heaven or hell they would ever get back together…that she'd met someone else.

She'd left out the part about Gunnar breaking things off. In that moment she'd clean forgotten. Looking at Javid, she'd known without question that her heart was and probably always would be Gunnar's!

She sighed at the sky. OK, so she'd been living in a bit of a fantasy, thinking they could actually make things work—and not just because of the whole children issue. She had a life to live elsewhere! Not that she could fathom going back to New Zealand, really, when there was so much going on here. She'd built something here for herself, regardless of Gunnar.

A few people were looking her way from the other side of the pond. Raising her hand, she half expected a scowl or a scathing remark, but the group of teenagers just waved back and smiled awkwardly, as if they'd seen a celebrity. Gunnar was so paranoid it had rubbed off on her!

After walking home, she hid behind the wall outside her apartment for a moment, till the man with the camera looked the other way. Then she darted to the door, jiggled the key in the lock, praying she wouldn't be snapped, and hated herself for caring at all.

It was only Gunnar who cared. And Javid, now.

Javid's own jealousy and ego had sent him to the airport. He'd known all along she was in Iceland, but he'd only flown here after seeing her photo with Gunnar. Typical. He didn't even know who Gunnar was.

The sight of his jet-lagged face last night, first furious and scathing, and then begging, crying and pleading, trying to block her from leaving his hotel room, had just made her angry instead of wanting to cower under a table. He'd dropped to the floor broken, a mess, but he'd agreed to sign the papers—finally. She'd almost wanted to feel sorry for him. But all she'd been thinking about was how he wasn't a part of her life any more. And neither was Gunnar.

Some hours later, Mahlia was between emails with her solicitor when a shriek from outside caught her ears. Suddenly several people were yelling, gathering outside, and Mahlia's heart almost bottomed out when she craned her neck on the balcony to look at the mountain range.

The volcano, far in the distance, which just last week had been largely inconspicuous, disguised as a harmless mountain, was now spitting fire. A thick cloud of steam and smoke rose faster than she could contemplate, threatening to blot out the sun.

The sky was turning darker and darker, and Mahlia felt a chill run through her as she took the stairs two at a time down to the street, glancing around. People were starting to evacuate, loading cars with whatever they could carry, running inside their homes to grab what they'd need. Dogs barked and children whimpered in confusion while she just stared at the mountains, realising there were probably people out there, *up* there...

The volcano was erupting, spewing molten lava and ash high into the air like a firework display. It was surreal.

Already her phone was ringing off the hook.

CHAPTER FOURTEEN

ERIK, ÁSTA AND Gunnar were in a huddle when she swerved into the hangar and hurried from her car.

'You're here.' Ásta pulled her into a quick one-armed hug.

She was panicked, which put Mahlia even more on edge, but she straightened up—not least because Gunnar was staring at her. He looked tired.

'Thanks for coming,' Gunnar said gruffly, and her heart panged just at seeing his narrowed eyes, the way he shoved his hands harder into his pockets.

Erik and Gunnar had already gathered intel. The eruption had sent a slow flow of lava spilling down the south-eastern side of the volcano, and the mayor of Reykjavik was in danger of getting trapped at the research base he was visiting with the scientists. They were still up there, in an area that would soon become inaccessible or swallowed by lava.

Mahlia's heart raced as she looked from Erik to Gunnar, then back again. Behind them more volunteers were loading vehicles with supplies, organising themselves into groups to head there by land and in helicopters.

'What about the villagers?' she asked as they headed towards Sven, who was hauling several boxes of water and supplies into the chopper.

'Some of them have already evacuated,' Gunnar said, hauling up another crate.

'Yeah, and some of them think their prayers will keep them safe,' Erik followed up.

Gunnar didn't touch her or talk to her as they boarded the chopper.

As they flew closer to the danger zone, the air felt thick and hot. The winds were picking up ash and debris all around them, visibility was decreasing rapidly, and every minute brought them closer to potential disaster...

What if they couldn't reach them in time?

It didn't bear thinking about.

Gunnar started working with the winch equipment and Mahlia's heart rose to her throat. She took his arm suddenly, leaning in over the roar of the blades. Hair whipped furiously around their faces as he partially opened the door and peeked out, sending ash inside to swirl between them. His gaze lowered to her fingers. She was clutching his arm tighter by the second.

'You wouldn't go down unless it was totally one hundred percent safe, would you?' she said, trying and probably failing to keep the emotion from her face.

He stared at her. 'Nothing about this is safe.'

She rolled her eyes. 'I know, but…'

'Nothing's going to happen to me. Or you. OK?'

His eyes drilled into her and she fumbled for words—professional words…words that might befit the current unprecedented situation—but he got in first.

'Why didn't you tell me Javid was here?' he said, stepping into a fire-retardant suit, yanking the zip up roughly.

She sat back, stunned. How did he know Javid was here?

'I saw it on your phone,' he said to her, reaching for the harness, tightening the belt around his waist. 'Before you left. You didn't tell me he was in the country. Did you think I'd try and stop you seeing him. Was that it?'

Mahlia gaped, feeling Ásta's eyes on her as she looked over a map of the area. Was that why he'd broken it off so fast? He could have told her…so she could have explained.

'I didn't know he was coming till I'd already left. He saw us in those photos and he flew here.

But, yes, I went to see him. I told him what I had to, and he's signing the papers.'

Gunnar looked shocked. 'Well…good.'

'Anyway, you didn't tell me your father was here!' she continued, raising her voice above the roaring blades. 'You really don't trust me at all, do you? You don't trust me with your family, and you don't trust me to make my own mind up about my own future!'

He shook his head. 'You want what I can't give you.'

'I only want *you*!'

She almost crumpled into him, but his eyes held hers now, and she swallowed a sob. This was pointless! He did know her, and he knew a part of her did still want a family, to be a mother. She always would…even if she willingly sacrificed the chance for him.

'At least I thought I did. I don't know, Gunnar.'

He said nothing, and she bit her tongue as he yanked on thick rubber boots.

'I didn't know my father was coming back,' he said eventually, 'not till this morning. That was news to me, too.'

She stared at him, grappling for words as the sequence of events started slotting into place. 'But you went to see him and the world didn't fall apart, did it? And you're here now, risking your life for others all over again, because your past isn't what's important.'

His jaw shifted this way and that as he held her eyes. Her legs were shaking with adrenaline. She could see his thoughts churning, something weakening, but then he seemed to brush it off, as if he didn't want to think about it. He tugged at the straps of the harness, then dragged his hands through his hair. She forced her mouth shut, cursing herself. She wanted to say the future was more important…the *only* thing that mattered. But his silence said it all.

She should book a flight home as soon as this mission was over, she thought defeatedly. Reassess, deal with the divorce with a clear head—not distract herself with someone she couldn't have.

'The research centre is there.'

Erik stuck his arm out to point between them, and she sucked a breath in, followed his finger. They were approaching the side of the volcano now, and the tiny research centre where the mayor and the scientists were trapped looked like nothing more than a series of shacks from up here. The spilling lava had already curled around the buildings, blocking the path for a rescue by land.

Despite the imminent danger, the sight was breathtaking. How could something so beautiful be so deadly?

Whenever the smoke cleared the molten lava glowed a brilliant orange-red against the deep hues of the ever-darkening ash-laden sky. Bright sparks flew off like fireflies as it spilled and spread like red treacle. It looked almost alive, with its own powerful energy, creating poker-like new paths for itself as it seeped and bubbled forward. Some trees had been charred black by fire, and whole sections of land had been swallowed up by molten rock already.

'How many people are down there?' she asked, sudden dread pooling in her stomach at just how close the lava was trickling to the research centre.

'They just confirmed five,' Erik said, his voice gruff with worry. 'I'll drop a cable once you get them out. The mayor is asthmatic, and with this smoke... We're the closest team already—the only chance they have right now.'

'I'll bring him up first,' Gunnar said. 'Mahlia, get ready.'

For a second too long she held his gaze, searching for a hint of the man who'd made love to her so passionately. He looked almost pained as he pulled his eyes away, and she swallowed back the urge to tell him to be careful. He was already pulling away, trying to push her out of his life. She should keep a shred of dignity and accept it.

This trip had never been about *him* anyway. At least, it had never been *supposed* to be…

Ásta shook her shoulder gently, urging her away from the door. Gunnar co-ordinated with Sven from the cockpit, checked the winch line with Erik, then shoved oxygen masks into his pack as they hovered closer. Below, Mahlia could just make out arms waving from a skylight in the observatory at the research centre, and her heart leapt as she grabbed up her backpack, ready to go with Gunnar.

'Stay here,' he commanded her.

She felt a jolt to her heart as Gunnar shoved the door further open, pulling his oxygen mask on tightly. The wind buffeted through her hair and dust and ash filled her lungs as he met her eyes one last time. In a heartbeat the clouds consumed him, and then he was gone.

The smoke was so thick it was more like a wall, but Gunnar kept going, forging through the ash towards the research centre. His lungs burned against his ribs and his heart pumped in his ears as he tried to breathe and stay calm. The steel shack that was the research centre was only metres away from where he'd landed, but the air around him was hot and toxic, and he could feel the intensity of the heat even from this distance, singeing his cheeks around the oxygen mask.

Above him, the chopper wove through a barrage of ash and debris, and he pictured Mahlia, gripping the doorframe, watching out for his return.

He'd pushed her away again... Why did he keep on doing that? Demus had got all up in his head on the phone, on his way to the hangar, telling him to keep Mahlia safe, that she was the best thing ever to have happened to him.

He *knew* that, he thought, glancing up as another chopper hovered into sight, then another, and another. Some were full of photographers and news correspondents. He couldn't escape them even on the side of a damn volcano.

The main door to the research centre was blocked by a massive lava rock boulder. He shouted to the guys they'd seen in the observatory. There was no way he could get into their line of vision, and the other door was blocked already by more huge black boulders. Heaving against their weight, he started to try and move it, picturing the much-loved mayor in there, feeling more ashamed than ever of how he'd treated Mahlia before he'd ordered her not to come down with him.

His old demons had come out in force, convincing him she was going to leave him like Idina had, and he'd made every excuse under the sun to himself as to why he was wrong for her—including the whole children thing. Was that really what he wanted? To be alone in life?

'Stop focusing on problems that don't even exist or your whole life is going to pass you by. Look at me and Inks. If we can make it work, then you can!' his brother had urged.

Demus saw through him and all his excuses, of course. He didn't deserve a brother like him, Gunnar thought, urging the boulder to move, cursing when it still didn't budge. And he probably didn't deserve Mahlia either, the way he'd just spoken to her. He'd messed up. She hadn't even seen that Javid was in Iceland when she'd asked him for a car back to Reykjavik from the cabin! And she'd finally given the guy his marching orders in person, all by herself. That must've taken courage, considering how the guy had had her in an emotional stranglehold for the last seven years—and he, as her trusted colleague, winchman and lover, had just broken things off with her.

Damn, this boulder was not giving an inch!

He almost turned around in defeat, but suddenly Mahlia was behind him, running through the swirling ash straight towards him. His stomach did a somersault as he watched her jump over a pile of glowing rocks. The smell of sulphur filled his nose and for a second he saw the strangest image in his mind: a little version of

Mahlia, stubborn, determined, needing him despite trying her best to prove she didn't, him sweeping her up in his arms... A daughter?

The smoke must be getting to his head.

'Mahlia, you can't be here.'

Her mouth twisted with exasperation as she pulled out a rope. 'I made them let me come. I'll stay away from you after this, if that's what you want,' she said through her mask. 'We need to move fast, Gunnar.'

Her knuckles went white as she tightened the rope around the boulder, and together they heaved and tugged until the way was clear. Gunnar yanked at the heavy steel door, revealing their way in with an ominous creak.

'It's so dark...' Panting, Mahlia grabbed the back of his suit by the belt as they entered the pitch-black corridor.

'The generator's out,' he said, pulling out a flashlight and putting a hand out to steady her.

The air was filled with the echo of distant shouts for help as they felt their way around the walls towards the sound of the cries. She stumbled against a trolley full of glass vials and he caught her, holding the flashlight under his chin for a second, an inch from her eyes.

'I'm sorry I overreacted about Javid flying to Reykjavik,' he said.

Mahlia turned away from him, edging along the wall. 'You did overreact, yes.'

'But that doesn't change anything, Mahlia. You deserve a better future now he's out of your life. You shouldn't have to sacrifice your dreams for me…'

'Great—so now there's another man telling me what's best for me,' she huffed over her shoulder, stumbling again and righting herself. 'I'm flying back to New Zealand soon anyway.'

He could have kicked himself. 'Really? You've booked a flight already?'

She sighed. 'Not yet, but there's legal stuff to sort out there…and I probably won't be back. Not for a while at least.'

'Mahlia—'

His words were cut off. A huge rumble from overhead made Mahlia gasp, and they staggered into each other. He dropped the flashlight.

'What was that?' she asked, wide-eyed, just as the cries sounded out again.

This time they were close enough to gauge where they were coming from. Together they hurried the rest of the way, till the noise brought them to another giant steel door. Gunnar's radio squawked.

'Gunnar, this is Erik. We've got a problem. All entrances are blocked by lava so you'll need to get the mayor and the others out through the roof. It's too dangerous for you to go back the way you went in.'

Mahlia turned pale, but Gunnar steeled himself. He spoke into the radio for confirmation and then pushed at the door. It was stuck.

'It's probably locked now the power's out,' he said, banging on the door.

Sure enough, a man who sounded very panicked confirmed they could no longer open it. There were five people in there, including the mayor, who was probably the person they could hear coughing hoarsely.

'Time to get creative,' said Gunnar, his eyes darting around in search of a plan.

Urging Mahlia back a safe distance, he grabbed a metal pipe off a nearby wall. The stench of burning rock wafting down the corridor made his nostrils burn and his stomach lurch.

'Can you do this?' she asked him from the opposite wall, removing her mask, then coughing with the ash.

His heart swelled at the look on her face—the same one he'd seen in the chopper. She was trying not to appear fazed by the situation, but her voice was trembling with fear and uncertainty, and it made him want to pull her into him, ask her to stay, not to take that flight. *Ever*.

Maybe she was right in what she'd said before. His father had come back, Ma was getting help, and despite everyone knowing about all the ugly skeletons in his closet, the world hadn't ended. He was making the past into a bigger deal than it had to be. And because of that he was destroying his own future!

Gunnar steeled himself, gripped the pipe hard and slammed it with all his strength repeatedly into the bar across the door. Over and over. On the fourth or fifth blow the lock shattered into pieces and the door swung open.

They pushed at it with one hard shove, and his eyes took in the facility, full of strange machinery, and the researchers, who flocked towards them in relief. The mayor, whom Gunnar recognised instantly, dropped to his knees on the floor when he saw them, holding his chest.

Gunnar passed out oxygen masks as Mahlia helped the mayor up, sitting him on a chair. 'We need to get everyone out of here *now*,' she said, eyeing the glass dome of the observatory above them nervously. It was so high.

'The power outage has left the dome closed,' one of the scientists told them. 'I don't know how else we can get out!'

Gunnar met Mahlia's eyes, saw the look of despair she shot him. *No*. They would *not* be stuck in here, waiting for a river to molten lava to snake in and swallow them—not if he could help it.

Casting his eyes around, he saw his answer—
the ventilation system.

'See the ventilation system up there?' he said,
racing for the ladder against the wall. 'That was
obviously installed before the dome. Maybe we
can climb up into the shafts.'

'Maybe?' someone said doubtfully.

Gunnar ignored him.

'How do we get up there?' the mayor managed to ask.

Gunnar pushed the ladder against a shelving
unit and shone the flashlight up, squinting against
the thick smoke as one of the scientists produced
a map of the system.

Shoving items from the desk to the floor,
Mahlia spread it out on the table. 'We *can* climb
up into the shafts,' she said. 'The map shows
there's a way out to the left, if we head through
the ventilation system.'

The mayor had started coughing and splutter-
ing so hard he could barely breathe. He tumbled
from the chair, gasping for breath. Mahlia raced
over to help him put his mask back on, throwing
Gunnar a look that said *Hurry!*

Gunnar took the ladder three rungs at a time.
It barely reached the vent they'd all have to fit
through, but he was ready. Opening out the rope
ladder he'd just yanked from his backpack, he
made quick work of fastening it to the bottom

of the vent. Soon it swung the whole way to the ground.

'Use the metal ladder to get onto the rope one. I'll pull you all up,' he called down.

Mahlia tried to make the mayor go first, but to Gunnar's dismay he refused.

'*They* should go first,' he insisted, gesturing to the team.

The scientists didn't argue with him.

'Hurry—one by one…climb up to me,' he instructed, as the first one took to the ladder.

Eyeing the space around him, he prayed it would hold them all and that there was a way out. He was crouching in the entrance to a long ventilation shaft. The end of the shaft had been made slightly wider—evidence that at some point this space *had* been planned as an escape route? He only hoped no one had sealed up the other end…

From the corridor below, an ominous groaning sound told him the building was far from stable now. One side of it—the side they'd entered from—was likely already engulfed in the lava.

'Gunnar, we're right above you. Can you see a way out?'

Erik's grave voice over the radio made his heart buck wildly as the first of the researchers reached him. His supposition was correct—he just knew it, he thought, straining his arms to pull the man up.

'Go! Go as far down the shaft as you can,' he told him as the second scientist almost fell from the ladder.

Mahlia ran to steady it.

Soon, the mayor and Mahlia were the only ones left in the lab below.

'Mahlia, I need you up here first,' he told her.

She wasted no time obeying him, for once, and when she was safely at his side he scrambled past her, climbing back down. The mayor was so weak that Gunnar had to carry him over his shoulder up the rope ladder, and Mahlia helped him pull the heavy, panting man into the shaft, where he tumbled into a heap against them, apologising.

'I know who you are,' he told Gunnar, breathing raggedly against Mahlia's shoulder.

He clutched Gunnar's collar in his fist for a second, hauling him closer, as if for inspection, and for a beat Gunnar wondered if the man might just shove him backwards from the shaft, down to the ground, and let the lava take him.

To his shock, the mayor mumbled, 'Thank you, Gunnar Johansson. Even if we die in here, you will die a hero for your bravery.'

'We are not going to die in here, sir,' Gunnar told him firmly, prising his hand away from his suit, praying that was true as he pulled out a compass.

'The map said that way,' Mahlia told him, without even looking at it.

She was right.

'Let's go,' he told her, ushering her along the shaft, taking the left turn, making sure the mayor was between them. The shaft was just big enough to be used as a crawl space, but the air was thick, more acrid than ever. Everyone was coughing now, despite their masks. The heat of lava burning through the walls and floors spurred them further forward, until finally a sliver of light appeared ahead.

Thank God!

His radio buzzed. Erik was asking where they were. His heart was like a drum as he explained as best he could. The building was now on weak foundations. They had to make it all the way outside before it was engulfed—only who knew how much time they had left?

Fumbling onwards on all-fours, he reached for the metal grate. With a strangled cry and a prayer, he pulled at one side of the thick iron bars, coughing against the smoke. Mahlia came up beside him and pulled on the bars with every ounce of strength she had, but his heart sank like a rock in his chest as they tugged and tugged together to no avail.

The grate just wouldn't move. They were stuck.

CHAPTER FIFTEEN

MAHLIA'S BODY WAS fighting to empty her stomach. She knew the shaft's exit was embedded into the side of the volcano. The heat scorched her skin, and the smell of burning rock was overwhelming now. It had already taken every bit of strength she possessed to help the struggling mayor through the shaft without injury, and now this...

She heaved at the grate again with Gunnar, watching the veins in his neck strain against the impossible task. She could see the ominous orange glow of lava snaking less than twenty metres away from them. With her hands burning, and the mayor of Reykjavik floundering behind her, she threw Gunnar a helpless look. The chopper was hovering noisily above, but they were on the brink of being devoured.

Was *this* how she was going to die? Next to Gunnar, at odds with Gunnar, having never even said the words *I love you*?

She did love him, she thought wryly as the

smoke tickled her already bone-dry throat. More than anything. For all the good it had done her. Why the hell had she told him she was definitely flying home to New Zealand, with no plans to return any time soon? OK, so she'd decided to do that in a snap decision, but she knew she'd only be running away again. Hurting him before he could hurt her more.

Now she knew what love—real love—felt like. It had never felt possible till Gunnar came along. She would probably never get over him, but at least going forward she'd have more confidence in the fact that she could love and be loved without suffocating or losing herself.

'Gunnar...' she started helplessly, blinking through the tears in her eyes she slumped backwards against the wall.

The second she hit it, she reeled back in pain.

Gunnar reached for her. 'What is it?'

Something hard was digging into her thigh. Gasping in relief, she yanked out the metal pipe Gunnar had used earlier, to bash down the door. He'd thrown it to the ground before grabbing the ladder, but she'd shoved it into the backpack, just in case.

Gunnar's eyes widened.

'Can you get us out with this?' she asked.

Behind him the team of researchers watched nervously, holding their hands over their masks.

The mayor had his eyes closed, praying in Icelandic between coughs and sucks on his inhaler.
At least he had one with him.

'I won't have the strength on my own, we'll
all have to help,' Gunnar told her quietly, and
she nodded, pressing a palm to his cheek without thinking.

He'd lifted every single one of these men sin-
gle-handedly from the rope ladder up into the
shaft, and then carried the mayor! Quickly, she
ordered everyone to get behind them and take a
part of the pipe, creating one long tool that hopefully, they could power enough between them.

Together they hammered at the rusty iron bars
till her joints felt like jelly, hearing the men stag-
ger and gasp, watching as the chopper's blades
spun against the ashen sky outside. The bars
creaked and groaned under the weight, but didn't
move. Erik was still urging them to hurry over
the radio. He'd sent down the winch line already.

'It's giving way…' Gunnar panted eventually,
as one of the hinges came apart.

She grinned ridiculously at the faint glimmer
of hope.

'One more time, Mahlia, everyone!,' he encouraged, gripping the other end of the pipe.

She gathered every last bit of energy left in
her exhausted body, and with everything she had
rammed at the grate with him, again and again,

until miraculously it sprang from both hinges, sending both her and Gunnar and two of the men behind them tumbling out onto the rocks. For a second she lay there, stunned and panting across his chest, his ash-streaked face less than an inch from her lips.

'That was close,' he said dryly, blinking.

Adrenaline made her laugh. His blue eyes smiled back into hers and she almost forgot they were at odds, almost kissed him in relief. But he hoisted her up to her feet, nodded towards the molten rock spewing from the volcano's crater, and darted back for the mayor.

The other men staggered out from the shaft one by one, shaking themselves down. She ushered them away from the approaching lava flow towards the waiting winch line as the heat burned her cheeks and Gunnar scooped the mayor into his arms. The man was fading fast, but still he insisted the research team go first.

'*You* go first,' Gunnar told Mahlia quietly when he reached her.

Above them, Ásta was waving urgently from the chopper's open door.

'No, Gunnar…'

Panic almost stole her voice. Metres from where they stood, blazing hot red rocks rolled ominously closer, like living predators, making one of the researchers cry out in fear. It was almost too hot to think, but she couldn't leave him—not now. They were in this together.

'Mahlia, you need to go,' he urged, putting the mayor down carefully on the blackened ground. 'I need you up there. I'll send them up to you one by one. OK?'

She reluctantly agreed, but she was far from OK as he helped her with the harness, then signalled to Ásta and Erik.

'Gunnar, I...' she started, grappling for words even as the volcano spewed another shower of lava behind him. 'I'm not going anywhere.' She was suddenly desperate to retract her words. 'I mean, I don't have to leave, Gunnar. Not if you feel the same way I do. I wasn't expecting you. I didn't ask for any of this. But I've spent the last seven years feeling like I can't speak my truth, so I'm saying it now, out loud, even if it's scarier than this!' She gestured around them at the blazing landscape. 'I love you, I want you, and I won't let you push me away—children or no children. We can work something out.'

He studied her eyes, clicking the last strap of the harness into place, and for a moment it was just the two of them.

'You *are* good for me,' she continued as the blades whirled the ash around her. 'I don't care about anything else and I'll prove it to you, even if it takes for ever.'

Pain flashed across his face for a second as he glanced upwards, and her heart lurched in response. 'Save yourself, Mahlia,' was all he said.

She didn't have time to vocalise anything else before a giant roar tore their eyes from each other. The research centre was collapsing behind them. It seemed as if the entire island was shaking with the force, and every breath she took was smoke and sulphur.

He tugged on the line with urgency. The wind whipped her face and tore at her hair as she strained to keep her eyes on him in the chaos, but soon all she could see was ash as she was hauled away from him up into the sky.

Gunnar watched her go, clenching his jaw as she disappeared into the dirty sky, hopping back from the rolling debris, urging the men up to a higher platform of dangerously wobbly rocks. He couldn't believe he'd just frozen—but what was he meant to say in response to that? All of her heart on display, on the line, for *him*. He'd shut down cold, even as she'd dangled right in front of him, in a situation like this.

God…he was such an idiot!

His head reeled as he waited for the line to reappear. He wanted to trust her more than anything. She truly thought that they could be more together than he was alone, a lonely one-man island, drifting through life in a sea of people who didn't even see him. Not the way she did. Maybe Mahlia really didn't care if any future children carried his name; maybe all she wanted was for *both* of them to stop putting up all these walls right now. She'd let hers come down, but him… He'd been hiding away where no one could stamp down on his heart for so long it was second nature for him to keep on believing his own excuses and creating new ones.

All he'd wanted to say to her just now was *I love you*, or *I need you too*, but he'd squished it down hard under his stupid pride and fear. He was so afraid of losing her the way he'd lost Idina that he was losing her anyway.

The winch line was back, swinging his way.

He shouted above the roar of the blades for the research team to get into the harness one by one. He'd have to stay on the ground; there was no point taking them up and down each time by himself. The air above him was too thick— he'd choke before he got them all into the chopper. They scrambled towards him, fear evident in their eyes—especially the mayor's. But the man still insisted the scientists all go before him.

'Mr Mayor, I don't think that's wise. Mahlia and the team are waiting up there to help you!'

'Everyone's going to need help after this,' he

told him, banging on his chest and sucking on his inhaler again.

Gunnar frowned, but determination took control of his tired limbs as he sent the men up towards Mahlia, working more quickly than he'd ever worked before. He muttered words of encouragement the whole time, even as his brain churned, hoping he wasn't showing a shred of the panic and doubt that were threatening to choke him more than the smoke.

The lava was creeping closer still… In minutes it would be licking at his heels like an eager pet if he didn't get up into that chopper.

The other helicopters were swirling above—news reporters, probably. Everyone wanted to see them get the mayor away from this disaster zone. Tears ran down the other men's faces as they expressed their wobbly gratitude, all of which he brushed away.

They weren't out of danger yet—not completely. But as soon as they were he would tell Mahlia he wanted her to stay, he decided. For ever. The thought of letting her down and seeing her walk away was crippling. He was a better man with her here, in every single way. He could even be a father, he realised, if she was with him. He'd been telling himself he didn't want children of his own, but that had been his fear talking too. They could do anything together.

Suddenly, he wanted nothing more than to see her walking down an aisle towards him, carrying his babies, cooking up a storm next to him at the cabin with their kids running around them… What the hell would he do if he couldn't have all that now?

'Gunnar, send him up!' Erik was ready for the mayor.

Gunnar clicked the last strap of the harness into place and for a moment it was just the two of them. The mayor nearly crushed his hand with a tight grip that defied his current state of health.

'I owe you my life, Dr Johansson,' he said gravely as the wind whipped his grey hair into a puffball. 'Don't think I'll forget this.'

Gunnar nodded as the winch line lifted the other man off the ground. The lava stream was almost too close for comfort now. He skipped along the rocks, away from it, waiting for the line to come back down. But just as he spotted it through the ash a giant rumble sent him to the ground. His radio went flying.

A shower of rocks had loosened and were rolling towards him, sending up so much soot and ash he couldn't see a thing. Holding his arms above his head for protection, he fumbled for the radio, straining his eyes against zero visibility. The winch line was nowhere in sight. He pushed himself off the ground and staggered forward, blindly feeling for it in all directions. The heat of the lava radiated behind him, almost unbearable.

He knew he had minutes at most before he was consumed by molten rock, and it was Mahlia's face he saw in his mind's eye as he prayed for a miracle.

The mayor was wheezing—everyone was now— but no one could speak, knowing Gunnar was still down there.

'Do you see him?' Mahlia asked Erik, doing her best to appear as if she wasn't completely breaking down on the inside. Her clothes were black, her face was thick with filthy dirt, and her heart was screaming out to Gunnar to tug on the rope and tell them he was OK.

'His radio's out,' Erik replied, trying him again.

Mahlia swallowed back a desperate sob. This was inconceivable. Gunnar was still down there, obviously unable to find the line in all the chaos and smoke. The mayor was coughing and retch-ing in the thick air and Sven was still circling over the spot where they'd pulled the team up. But it was almost too hot to breathe now; her lungs felt ragged.

'We have to wait,' Mahlia begged, seeing Ásta and Erik throwing looks at each other. They didn't think… Surely, they didn't think he was already dead? 'We can't leave him down there. Let me go back down there.'

Ásta caught her arm, then gripped her hand. 'No, Mahlia.'

She was shaking. 'But we can't just leave him. He might be… He's *waiting* for us.'

A pause.

'Gunnar would want us to get out of here,' Erik said gravely, still watching the line. 'We have all these people who need attention and we're running low on fuel.'

Beneath them, the research centre had now been swallowed whole, and the river of lava glimmered ominously where they'd just been standing. Mahlia could barely think straight.

'There are other teams on the mountain… everyone will be looking for him,' Ásta told her reassuringly, but Mahlia knew what she was really thinking.

Gunnar was already gone.

It was all she could do not to scream. Had she really lost him for ever? Oh, God… Oh, God, how would she cope? And how was she going to break it to Demus?

The hangar was hive of activity when they landed. Sirens wailed in the distance, while several ambulances and other rescue trucks were parked on the concrete in the floodlights, already attending to the injured people who'd made it off the mountain. News reporters were swarming all around them, asking about the mayor, asking about Gunnar, but Mahlia just trembled against Ásta's shoulder as they let the paramedics take over their stunned researchers.

Ásta drew her close. 'It's going to be OK.'

Nothing is ever going to be OK again, she felt like saying.

It felt as if the bottom had just fallen out of her world—as if the life had been sucked right out of her. She'd finally told him exactly how she felt, finally stopped cowering behind her own fears. Whether her feelings were reciprocated or not, at least she'd told him… And now she'd never see his face again.

Tears welled up in her eyes as she tried to process it all. She'd taken a risk, told him exactly what she wanted, despite her fear that he wouldn't feel the same way, wouldn't respond in kind, but it hadn't been enough. Nothing would bring him back.

Then came a voice.

'Mahlia…'

Mahlia's head snapped up. Gunnar was standing in front of her, blackened and weary, a look of pure relief on his face.

For a second, she blinked in disbelief. He was alive!

'Gunnar!'

Ásta released her and started crying into her hands, but Mahlia ran for him, barely believing her eyes as Gunnar caught her mid-stride. She sobbed into his chest. The news reporters were clamouring around them now, but for once he didn't seem to care; he kept his focus solely on her, not letting her go for a single second.

'I'm so sorry,' he told her, speaking into her hair. 'All I wanted the second I sent you up there was to tell you that I love you, too. I want everything you want, and I want us to make this work.'

'I thought I'd lost you,' she said, her voice coming out strangled.

'One of the news choppers threw me a line,' he told her wryly, pressing his hands to her face, scrunching up her hair, kissing her. 'Who'd have thought it? Mahlia, I wasn't ever going to give up on us. I fell in love with you a long time ago. I just didn't know what to do with my feelings, or if I could give you what you needed…what I need too. You know…' He paused. 'I never thought children were for me, but then I met you and everything started to change…'

Mahlia almost laughed. 'What I need most is for you to love me, and to let me love *you*, and let that be enough for us both.'

'And it will be. For now.'

Gunnar's eyes shone with so much love and hope she almost burst.

'I can really see myself as a dad. In fact, I can see myself doing a lot of things with you I never thought I'd get to experience. But life is short, and we need to grab every opportunity we can to make the most of it.'

'Life is *too* short,' she whispered.

Mahlia couldn't even speak any more. Instead, she kissed him back, as the circle of press and onlookers grew wider and his arms around her grew tighter.

He was still holding her tightly in his arms when the mayor was wheeled over to them in a chair, seemingly determined to address the press while in the same shot as Gunnar.

Mahlia moved to step away, frantically wiping the tears from her face, but Gunnar held on to her hand, pulled her closer to his side, and made sure to kiss the top of her head tenderly in front of the cameras. Whatever parts of her that hadn't already been singed in the day's heat melted.

The mayor cleared his throat and stood, pressing a hand to Gunnar's shoulder as he did his best to recount in his own words how they'd helped them all to escape from the research centre before it collapsed.

'Tonight, I stand here very much alive, in awe of these brave men and women who risk their own lives to save the people of Iceland. I want to thank you and your team, Dr Johansson, on live television, so that all of Iceland knows how much I personally applaud and appreciate your courage and dedication. You've done your country proud tonight. We will never forget this moment.'

The mayor went on to praise Mahlia. Covered in dust, and still drawing breath through his inhaler, he concluded his speech by proclaiming that from this day forward they would be known as heroes throughout the country.

Mahlia almost laughed as excitement and happiness bubbled through her, and when the audience erupted into a standing ovation her chest swelled with joy. Gunnar looked quite shellshocked, standing in stoic silence beside her, but he never let go of her fingers. She knew he was showing all of Iceland that they were together, trusting that she wouldn't run from the consequences—not that they could be anything but positive after this.

The applause and cheering almost caused her eardrums to burst as the mayor was wheeled away towards a waiting ambulance, and people Mahlia had never even seen before moved in to embrace her and thank her.

She caught Gunnar's eyes as the cameras clicked away, capturing every second. He held her hand through every question she went on to answer, about who she was, how she was the founder of the e-bike company that had recently thrown Demus Johansson back into the spotlight, and how, yes, she was also Gunnar's girlfriend.

'She's more than that,' he said then, facing the cameras. 'She's the love of my life.'

And as he kissed her again, despite the chaos, Mahlia had the most delicious, all-consuming feeling that everything was going to be just fine for her and Gunnar. More than fine…

EPILOGUE

One year later

MAHLIA STOOD ATOP a cliff overlooking the North Atlantic, her heart racing with anticipation. The sun was setting on the horizon, casting its rosy hue across the rocky shoreline and painting Gunnar's handsome face golden. He had taken her to the most romantic location in Iceland, and she could sense he was distracted and twitchy as he took her hand in his and led them slowly down onto the secluded beach, where several people were riding horses across the sparkling black sand.

Gunnar smiled down at her and then dropped to one knee.

Wait... What?

Mahlia gasped, almost dropping down onto her own knees in front of him. She'd been right. He was planning to propose.

'Gunnar...'

He pulled a small velvet box from his pocket,

opened it up, and she could barely see the exquisite antique diamond ring through the tears in her eyes.

'Mahlia, you know I love you with all my heart. This past year has been the best year of my life, and I'm in awe of everything you are, everything you do. Will you marry me?'

He was looking at her with so much admiration Mahlia couldn't believe it. She was stunned into silence for a moment before she managed to say a thing.

'Gunnar, yes. I will absolutely marry you!'

Tears streamed down her face as she pulled him to her in the last remaining streaks of glistening sunlight. How a person could love someone more than she loved him was hard to imagine, she thought, as he slid the ring onto her finger.

With Iceland now her adopted home, language lessons taking up three nights a week and her e-bike company flourishing, she was beyond thankful for how far they had come together over the past year…how much they had done.

Gunnar was a changed man. Ever since they'd given in to their feelings for each other and committed to starting again, together, he had been not just the partner she'd always dreamed of, he had thrown himself into everything the community asked of him, and was using his notoriety to create a whole new legacy—with her.

'Demus will kill me for not getting your acceptance on camera,' he said to her now, as she wiped at her eyes and kissed him.

'We don't have to share everything we do with the world,' she told him, smiling, studying the stunning ring in astonishment.

She was lucky to be spending these precious moments with him this week. He'd been in hospital for what felt like days on end already, with his kidney patients—not that they didn't try to make the most of every second of their spare time together.

'Besides, I'm sure he and Inka are waiting with some cocktails and canapés or something somewhere—am I right?'

'You are correct.' Gunnar grinned. 'But would you mind if we go and see my mother first?' he asked. 'She deserves to be the first to know.'

Mahlia drew his hands into hers and squeezed them tight as three women on horses trotted past and held up their hands at them, smiling in recognition.

Kaðlín Johansson was doing so much better now, almost a whole year sober, and Mahlia was humbled to have been invited into her world since her release from rehab. After Gunnar's father had left again, for Greece, the family had at last put most of their struggles behind them, and she and Gunnar spent every Sunday with his

mother, Demus and Inka, at her newly renovated
home. The bond she'd rekindled with her sons
had got her thinking a lot about her own family, and she was excited to be flying her parents
over again soon—the first time they'd met Gunnar had been magical.

'I know we have a lot to plan, but I was thinking Demus should drive an adapted vehicle to
bring us to the church,' Gunnar said now, walking with her along the sand, the wind whipping
up his shaggy hair beside her.

She nodded, smiling to herself. So he'd been
thinking about this for a while, then. The idea
didn't surprise her; he was now as much involved
in her venture as Demus. In fact, he and Gunnar
had applied for government grants to develop pi-
oneering solutions for sustainable living across
the country. Their team was building solar-pow-
ered charging stations across rural villages, as
well as helping to develop innovative ways to
harvest energy from glaciers and other natural
forces to provide clean power sources.

They were becoming known across Iceland for
their eco-initiatives, as much as Gunnar's life-
changing surgeries, and between his new ven-
tures and her e-bike events there wasn't a party
in Reykjavik they weren't invited to.

Not that they attended them all.

It was nice relaxing at the cabin, just the two

of them. And one day soon they'd be three, she thought with a misty smile, touching a hand to her belly.

She'd fallen pregnant a month ago. It had been a little nerve-racking, telling Gunnar, just in case he had any lingering reservations, but he'd lifted her up and spun her around in the kitchen and seemed as excited as a child who'd just been told he'd be getting a new puppy.

He'd reassured her once again that he was definitely ready to be a father, and that he couldn't wait to make the announcement—although just to their families for now. She'd been so relieved she'd actually cried down the phone to her mother, and again in front of his.

They *would* be the best parents. She knew it. She could feel it. Their children would be loved by everyone—not just them.

And now, she thought in excitement, staring at the orange sun sinking into the sea, they had a wedding to plan, too. And *this* marriage was going to last for ever.

* * * * *